ME and EARL and the Dying GIRL

AMULET BOOKS
NEW YORK

ME

and EARL

and the *Dying* GIRL

A NOVEL

JESSE ANDREWS

Library of Congress Cataloging-in-Publication Data

Andrews, Jesse.
Me & Earl & the dying girl / by Jesse Andrews.
p. cm.
ISBN 978-1-4197-0176-4
[1. Friendship—Fiction. 2. Leukemia—Fiction. 3. High schools—Fiction.
4. Schools—Fiction. 5. Family life—Pennsylvania—Fiction. 6. Jews—United States—Fiction. 7. Pittsburgh (Pa.)—Fiction. 8. Humorous stories.] I. Title.
II. Title: Me and Earl and the dying girl.
PZ7.A56726Me 2012
[Fic]—dc23
2011031796

Text copyright © 2012 Jesse Andrews

Book design by Chad W. Beckerman

The text in this book is set in 10.75-point Adobe Garamond.

Printed and bound in U.S.A.
10 9 8 7 6 5 4

ABRAMS
THE ART OF BOOKS SINCE 1949

115 West 18th Street
New York, NY 10011
www.abramsbooks.com

To Schenley, which Benson is not

A NOTE FROM GREG GAINES, AUTHOR OF THIS BOOK

I have no idea how to write this stupid book.

Can I just be honest with you for one second? This is the literal truth. When I first started writing this book, I tried to start it with the sentence "It was the best of times; it was the worst of times." I genuinely thought that I could start this book that way. I just figured, it's a classic book-starting sentence. But then I couldn't even figure out how you were supposed to follow that up. I stared at the computer for an hour and it was all I could do not to have a colossal freak-out. In desperation, I tried messing with the punctuation and italicization, like:

It was the *best* of times? *And* it was the worst of times?!!

What the hell does that even mean? Why would you even think to do that? You wouldn't, unless you had a fungus eating your brain, which I guess I probably have.

The point is, I have no idea what I'm doing with this book. And the reason for that is, I'm not a writer. I'm a filmmaker. So now you're probably asking yourself:

1. Why is this guy writing a book and not making a film?
2. Does it have to do with the brain-fungus thing?

Answer Key

1. I'm writing a book instead of making a film because I have retired from filmmaking forever. Specifically, I retired after making the Worst Film Ever Made. Usually the goal is to retire after making the best possible thing you can make—or, even better, die—but I did the opposite. A brief outline of my career would look like this:

    i. Many Bad Films
    ii. A Mediocre Film
    iii. Some OK Films
    iv. A Decent Film
    v. Two or Three Good Films
    vi. A Bunch of Pretty Great Films
    vii. The Worst Film Ever Made

Fin. How bad was that film? It killed someone, that's how bad it was. It caused an actual death. You'll see.

2. Let's just say that it would explain a lot of things if there were a fungus eating my brain. Although that fungus would have to have been eating my brain for basically my entire life. At this point it's possible that the fungus has gotten bored and left, or died from malnutrition or something.

I do actually want to say one other thing before we get started with this horrifyingly inane book. You may have already figured out that it's about a girl who had cancer. So there's a chance you're thinking, "Awesome! This is going to be a wise and insightful story about love and death and growing up. It is probably going to make me cry literally the entire time. I am so *fired up* right now." If that is an accurate representation of your thoughts, you should probably try to smush this book into a garbage disposal and then run away. Because here's the thing: *I learned absolutely nothing from Rachel's leukemia.* In fact, I probably became *stupider* about life because of the whole thing.

I'm not really putting this very well. My point is this: This book contains precisely zero Important Life Lessons, or Little-Known Facts About Love, or sappy tear-jerking Moments When We Knew We Had Left Our Childhood Behind for Good, or whatever. And, unlike most books in which a girl gets cancer, there are definitely no sugary paradoxical single-sentence-paragraphs that you're supposed to think are deep because they're in italics. Do you know what I'm talking about? I'm talking about sentences like this:

The cancer had taken her eyeballs, yet she saw the world with more clarity than ever before.

Barf. Forget it. For me personally, things are in no way more meaningful because I got to know Rachel before she died. If anything, things are *less* meaningful. All right?

So I guess we should just start.

(I just realized that you may not know what *"fin"* means. It is a filmmaking term. Specifically, it is French for "This movie is over, which is good, because it probably confused the hell out of you, because it was made by French people.")

Fin for real this time.

Chapter 1

HOW IT IS POSSIBLE TO EXIST IN A PLACE THAT SUCKS SO BAD

So in order to understand everything that happened, you have to start from the premise that high school sucks. Do you accept that premise? Of course you do. It is a universally acknowledged truth that high school sucks. In fact, high school is where we are first introduced to the basic existential question of life: **How is it possible to exist in a place that sucks so bad?**

Most of the time middle school sucks even worse, but middle school is so pathetic that I can't even bring myself to write about it, so let's just focus on high school.

All right. Allow me to introduce myself: Greg S. Gaines, seventeen. During the period described in this book, I was a senior at Benson High School in lovely inner-city Pittsburgh, Pennsylvania. And before we do anything else, it is necessary for us to examine Benson and the specific ways in which it sucks.

So, Benson is on the border of Squirrel Hill, an affluent neighborhood, and Homewood, a non-affluent neighborhood, and it draws about equal numbers of students from both. On television, it's usually the rich kids who assert control at a high

school; however, most of Squirrel Hill's genuinely rich kids go to the local private school, Shadyside Academy. The ones that remain are too few to impose any kind of order. I mean, occasionally, they try to, and that tends to be more adorable than anything else. Like when Olivia Ryan freaks out about the puddle of urine that appears in one of the stairwells most days between 10:30 and 11:00 AM, shrieking at bystanders in an insane, misguided attempt to try to figure out who did it. You want to say, "Liv! The perpetrator has probably not returned to the scene of the crime. Pee Diddy is long gone by now." But even if you did say that, she probably wouldn't stop freaking out. And anyway, my point is that the freak-out doesn't have any measurable effect on anything. It's like when a kitten tries to bite something to death. The kitten clearly has the cold-blooded murderous instinct of a predator, but at the same time, it's this cute little kitten, and all you want to do is stuff it in a shoebox and shoot a video of it for grandmas to watch on YouTube.

So the rich kids aren't the alpha group of the school. The next most likely demographic would be the church kids: They're plentiful, and they are definitely interested in school domination. However, that strength—the will to dominate—is also their greatest weakness, because they spend so much time trying to convince you to hang out with them, and the way they try to do that is by inviting you over to their church. "We've got cookies and board games," they say, or that sort of thing. "We just got a Wii set up!" Something about it always seems a little off. Eventually, you realize: These *same exact sentences* are also said by child predators.

So the church kids can never be the alpha group, either.

Their tactics are just too creepy. At many schools, the jocks would be a good bet to ascend to the throne, but at Benson, they're pretty much all black, and many of the white kids are afraid of them. Who else is there to lead the masses? The smart kids? Please. They have no interest in politics. They're hoping simply to attract as little attention as possible until high school is over. Then they can escape to some college where no one will mock them for knowing how an adverb works. The theater kids? My God, it would be a bloody massacre. They would be found beaten to death with their own dog-eared *The Wiz* songbooks. The stoners? Too lacking in initiative. The gangbangers? Too rarely on the premises. The band kids? It would be like with the theater kids, except somehow even sadder. The gothy dorks? Impossible even as a thought experiment.

So at the top of the Benson social hierarchy, there is a vacuum. The result: chaos.

(Although let me also note that I'm using overly simplistic categories here. Are there multiple separate groups of smart kids/rich kids/jocks/etc.? Yes. Are there a bunch of groups that don't have easy labels because they're just loose collections of friends without a single defining characteristic? Also yes. I mean, if you wanted, I could just map out the entire school for you, with geeky labels like "Middle-Class African American Junior Sub-Clique 4c," but I am pretty sure no one wants me to do that. Not even the members of Middle-Class African American Junior Sub-Clique 4c [Jonathan Williams, Dajuan Williams, Donté Young, and, until he got really serious about the trombone midway through junior year, Darnell Reynolds].)

So there are a bunch of groups, all jockeying for control, and consequently all of them want to murder each other. And so the problem is that if you're part of a group, everyone outside of that group wants to murder *you*.

But here's the thing. There's a solution to that problem: Get access to *every* group.

I know. I know. This sounds insane. But it's exactly what I did. I didn't *join* any group outright, you understand. But I got access to all of them. The smart kids, the rich kids, the jocks, the stoners. The band kids, the theater kids, the church kids, the gothy dorks. I could walk into any group of kids, and not one of them would bat an eye. Everyone used to look at me and think, "Greg! He's one of us." Or maybe something more like: "That guy's on our side." Or at the very least: "Greg is a guy who I am *not* going to flick ketchup at." This was a brutally difficult thing to accomplish. Consider the complications:

1. Infiltration of any one group must remain concealed to most, if not all, of the others. If rich kids observe you chatting amiably with goths, the gated community closes its doors to you. If church kids notice you stumbling out of a stoner car, cloaked in smoke as though exiting a sauna, your days of conscientiously not blurting out the F-word in the church basement are over. And if a jock, God forbid, witnesses you hobnobbing with theater kids, he will immediately assume you are gay, and there is no force on earth greater than the fear jocks have of homosexuals. None. It's like the Jewish fear of Nazis, except the complete opposite with regard to who is beating the crap out of whom. So I guess it's more like the Nazi fear of Jews.

2. You cannot become too deeply enmeshed in any one group. This follows from point one, above. One must instead be at the periphery at all times. Befriend the goths, but do not under any circumstances dress like them. Participate in band, but avoid their hour-long jam sessions in the band room after school. Make appearances at the church's ridiculously decked-out rec room, but shun any activity wherein someone is actively talking about Jesus.

3. At lunch, before school, and at all other times in public, you must keep an insanely low profile. I mean, just forget about lunch. Lunch is where you are asked to demonstrate your allegiance to one group or another by sitting with them for all to see—or, God forbid, being asked to sit with some poor sap who's not even *in* a group. It's not that I have anything against group-less kids, obviously. My heart goes out to them, the wretched bastards. In the chimpanzee-ruled jungle of Benson, they are the cripples, hobbling along on the forest floor, unable to escape harassment and torture from the others. Pity them, yes; befriend them, never. To befriend them is to share their fate. They try to hook you by saying things like, "Greg, d'you wanna sit with me." What they are really saying is: "Please hold still while I stab you in your legs, so that you cannot run when we are overtaken by the Biting Ones."

But really anytime you're in a room with a bunch of groups mixed together, you have to disengage as much as possible. In class, at lunch, wherever.

At this point, you may be asking: "But what about your friends? You can't ignore your friends if you're in class with them."

To which I say: Maybe you haven't been paying attention. The whole *point* is that you can't be friends with anyone. That's the tragedy and the triumph of this whole way of being that I'm talking about. **You can't lead a typical high school life.**

Because here's the thing: The typical high school life sucks.

You may also be asking: "Greg, why are you talking trash on the group-less kids? It sounds like *you're* basically a group-less kid." You have a point, sort of. The thing is, I was in no group, but I was also in every group. So you can't really describe me as group-less.

Honestly, there's no good word for what I was doing. For a while I thought of myself as a practitioner of High School Espionage, but ultimately that was too misleading of a term. That made it sound like I was sneaking around having illicit sexual liaisons with voluptuous Italian women. For one thing, Benson doesn't *have* any voluptuous Italian women. The closest thing we have is Ms. Giordano in the principal's office, and she's kind of lumpy and has a face like a parrot. Also, she does this thing women sometimes do with their eyebrows where they just completely shave them off and draw new ones in a different weird place with a Sharpie or something, and the more you think about it, the more your stomach starts churning around and you want to claw your own head.

That is literally the only appearance Ms. Giordano is going to make in this book.

Let's just move on.

Chapter 2

THE FIRST DAY OF SENIOR YEAR IN CONVENIENT SCRIPT FORMAT

So I guess we should start with the first day of senior year. Which was actually awesome until Mom got involved.

I mean, "awesome" is a relative term. My expectations were low, obviously. Maybe "awesome" is too strong a word. The sentence should be: "I was pleasantly surprised when the first day of senior year did not make me want to freak out and hide in my own locker pretending to be dead."

School is always stressful, and then the first day of any school year is especially insane because the hangout spots have to be realigned. I failed to note in the previous chapter that the traditional groups of Rich, Jock, Smart, Theater, etc., are further subdivided by grade: The sophomore gothy dorks live in resentful terror of the senior gothy dorks, the smart juniors are dismissive and mistrustful of the smart freshman, etc. So when a class moves out, all of the spots that they used to occupy before school are up for grabs, and there's usually some weirdness as a result.

Mainly it made for a busy morning for me. I showed up

stupidly early to see how things would play out, and there were already some kids staking out their ground. These tended to be representatives of Benson's more dicked-upon groups.

INT. HALLWAY IN FRONT OF THE LIBRARY —
MORNING

JUSTIN HOWELL is hovering nervously near
the door to the library, hoping to claim it
for the theater kids. He is pacing back and
forth humming THE THEME FROM *RENT* OR MAYBE
CATS. With visible relief, he notices GREG
approaching.

> JUSTIN HOWELL
> *clearly relieved that it is not a*
> *jock or gangbanger or anyone else*
> *who will immediately call him a*
> *faggot*
> Oh hi Greg.

> GREG GAINES
> Justin, good to see you.

> JUSTIN HOWELL
> Good to see *you*. Greg how was
> your *summer*.

                    GREG
It was hot and boring, and I
can't believe it's over
already.

                  JUSTIN HOWELL
HA HA HA HA HA HA HA HA HA.
OH HA HA HA HA HA HA HA HA HA HA
HA HA HA HA.

This seemingly innocuous JOKE has caused
Justin Howell to completely lose his shit.
Perhaps it is the MIND-DESTROYING ANXIETY
of being back at school.

Meanwhile, this was not quite the response
Greg was hoping to get. He had intended to
say something bland and unmemorable. Now
he is SHRUGGING and FIDGETING AWKWARDLY
and attempting to avoid EYE CONTACT, which
he usually does when people are laughing
at a thing that he has said.

                  JUSTIN HOWELL (CONT'D)
                  turning his eyebrows into
                  a weird shape
HA HA HA HA HA HA HA HA HA HA HA
HA HA HA.

MRS. WALTER, the librarian, arrives. She
is glaring at both of them. She is almost
definitely an ALCOHOLIC.

> JUSTIN HOWELL
> Hi Mrs. Walterrrr.

> MRS. WALTER
> *with dislike*
> Hhngh.

> JUSTIN HOWELL
> Greg that is *too funny.*

> GREG
> All right man, I'll see you later.

I was obviously not gonna go into that library and have a
lengthy bro-hang with Justin Howell, for reasons I've already
explained to you. It was time to move on.

INT. HALLWAY IN FRONT OF THE BAND ROOM —
MORNING

LAQUAYAH THOMAS and BRENDAN GROSSMAN have
not been let into the band room yet. Despite
not having instruments, they are poring
over some SHEET MUSIC. You can sort of tell

that they are doing this to show everyone
that they are good enough at music to just
casually sit around reading sheet music.

                    BRENDAN GROSSMAN
          Gaines. You doing orchestra this
          year?

                    GREG
                apologetically
          Couldn't fit it in.

                    BRENDAN GROSSMAN
          Whaaaaat.

                    LAQUAYAH THOMAS
                incredulously
          But you woulda got timpani this year!
          Now who's gonna play timpani?

                    BRENDAN GROSSMAN
                mournfully
          It's gonna be like Joe DiMeola.

                    GREG
          Yeah, probably Joe. He's a better
          percussionist than me anyway.

                    LAQUAYAH THOMAS
        Joe gets the sticks all sweaty.

                        GREG
        That's because he's so *focused*.

INT. AUDITORIUM — MORNING

Two senior gothy dorks, SCOTT MAYHEW and ALLAN
McCORMICK, are camped out in some seats near
the back playing Magic cards. GREG enters
cautiously, his eyes darting from side to side.
The auditorium is perhaps the school's most
valuable real estate. It is highly unlikely
that this little goth colony will survive the
WAVES OF JOCKS, THEATER KIDS, AND GANGBANGERS
that will doubtless arrive later this morning.

                        GREG
        Hello, gentlemen.

                    SCOTT MAYHEW
        Good day to you.

                    ALLAN McCORMICK
            blinking rapidly and forcefully
                for probably no reason
        Yes, good day.

The gothy dorky kids are very low in the social hierarchy, but at the same time they are almost impossible to infiltrate. Maybe it's *because* they're so low in the hierarchy. They're insanely suspicious of everyone who tries to talk to them. This is because pretty much all of their characteristics are targets of ridicule: their love of elves and dragons, their trench coats and long un-groomed or maybe-*too*-well-groomed hair, their habit of striding around way too fast while breathing really hard out of their noses. Getting them to accept you is difficult without *becoming* a gothy dork.

Actually, I feel kind of a soft spot for them because I completely understand their worldview. They hate high school, just like I do. They're constantly trying to escape it and instead live in a fantasy world where they can spend all their time striding around in the mountains, jabbing people with swords under the eerie light of like eight different moons or something. Sometimes I feel like, in an alternate universe, I could have *been* one of them. I'm pasty and chubby and completely insane in social situations. And if I'm being honest, attacking people with swords is awesome.

That was what I was thinking a little bit, crouching there with them in the auditorium. But then I had a realization.

SCOTT MAYHEW, after much deliberation, plays a CARD entitled "Horde of the Undead."

                    ALLAN McCORMICK
         Curses.

GREG

> Scott, great horde.

My realization was that I could never *actually* live a life where I had to be constantly doing things like praising a dude's horde.

So that made me feel better about myself.

It did not take me all that long to respectfully get the hell out of there.

INT. AREA IN FRONT OF THE SOUTH
STAIRWELL — MORNING

All four members of MIDDLE-CLASS AFRICAN
AMERICAN JUNIOR SUB-CLIQUE 4C are
positioned near the doors. Meanwhile, a
lone sophomore church kid, IAN POSTHUMA,
has spread his stuff farther down the hall
and is grimly waiting for REINFORCEMENTS.

This is a classic situation in which you try to engage people as little as possible, because if you look like you're part of one group, the other group will take notice and ostracize you. I mean, being ostracized by sophomore church kids would not be the worst thing in the world, but my one goal in life was to not be ostracized by *anyone*. Were there times when this goal seemed like the goal of a moron? Yes. But honestly, name one life goal that does not occasionally seem like the goal of a total moron. Even being president would completely suck, if you really give it any thought at all.

GREG gives IAN POSTHUMA a low-key head-
nod greeting. Then the RUBBER BALL that
JONATHAN WILLIAMS has been flinging against
RANDOM SURFACES ricochets into one of
GREG'S TEETH.

In previous years, there would have been no dignified way
to deal with this. The ball-throwing group would have burst
into raucous laughter, and my only course of action would have
been to stride briskly away, probably while being further pelted.

But pretty quickly, it became clear that this year, things
were different.

Instead of glorying in the fact that
his ball has bounced into GREG'S TOOTH,
JONATHAN WILLIAMS tucks his head into his
shirt with embarrassment.

> DARNELL REYNOLDS
> *visibly annoyed*
> I *told* you you would hit someone.

> DONTÉ YOUNG
> Dude's a senior.

> JONATHAN WILLIAMS
> *mumbling*
> Sorry.

```
                    GREG
        It's all good.


DAJUAN WILLIAMS gives Jonathan Williams a
shove.
                 DONTÉ YOUNG
            cleaning a fingernail
        Can't be throwing shit.
```

Basically, being a senior means that when people throw things at your teeth, it's accidental. In other words, being a senior is awesome.

All morning before school, and then all day, that was how things went. It was kind of a perfect day in that regard. I spent a few minutes in the parking lot with a gaggle of ill-tempered foreign kids led by Nizar the Surly Syrian, then exchanged some hellos with the soccer team, and this year none of them tried to grab and injure my nipples. Dave Smeggers, noted stoner, began telling me a long and excruciatingly pointless story about his summer, but was soon distracted by some birds, at which point I made my escape. Vonta King tried to get me to sit with him across from room 318, so I pretended I was on my way to a meeting with a teacher, and he accepted it without argument. And so on and so forth.

Also, at one point I almost walked into one of Madison Hartner's boobs. Her boobs are about at eye level for me.

Chapter 3

LET'S JUST GET THIS EMBARRASSING CHAPTER OUT OF THE WAY

For the purposes of this god-awful book, I have to talk briefly about girls, so let's see if we can get through that without me punching myself in the eyeball.

First things first: Girls like good-looking guys, and I am not very good-looking. In fact, I sort of look like a pudding. I am extremely pale and somewhat overweight. I have kind of a rat face, and my mediocre vision makes me squint a lot. Finally, I have what has been diagnosed as chronic allergic rhinitis, which sounds interesting but basically just means a constant booger problem. I can't really breathe through my nose, so most of the time my mouth is hanging open, which gives the appearance of major stupidity.

Second: Girls like confident guys. With that in mind, please reread the previous paragraph. It's hard to be confident when you look like a chubby, squinty, mentally defective rodent-human who picks his nose.

Third: My girl tactics need work.

Failed Girl Tactic #1: The Non-Crush. In fourth grade, I realized that girls were desirable. I had no idea what you were supposed to do with them, of course. I just sort of wanted to have one, like as a possession or something. And of all the fourth graders, Cammie Marshall was definitely the hottest. So I had Earl go up to Cammie Marshall on the playground and say: "Greg doesn't have a crush on you. But he's worried that you have a crush on him." I was standing about five feet away when Earl did this. The hope was that Cammie would say, "Secretly, I totally have a crush on Greg and want to be his girlfriend." Instead, she said, "Who?"

"Greg Gaines," said Earl. "He's standing right over there."

They both turned to look at me. I took my finger out of my nose to wave. That was when I realized that I had had my finger in my nose.

"Nope," said Cammie.

Things did not really improve from there.

Failed Girl Tactic #2: The Nonstop Insults. Cammie was obviously out of my league. But her best friend, Madison Hartner, was also pretty hot. In fifth grade, I figured Madison would be starved for attention, given that Cammie was so hot. (Note: In retrospect, at seventeen, it's hard to understand how a ten-year-old could be hot. At the time, though, this made perfect sense.)

Anyway, with Madison I used a tactic I had seen work for other fifth graders: insults. Constant vicious insults. Insults that didn't even make any sense: I called her Madison Avenue Hartner, not knowing what Madison Avenue was. Bad-ison. Fat-ison. It took me a while, but eventually I discovered Madison Fartner, which made some other kids giggle, so I used it all the time.

The thing was, I was relentless. I went way too far. I told her she had a tiny dinosaur brain and a second brain in her butt. I said her family didn't have dinner, they just sat around and farted at each other because they were too stupid to know what food was. At one point I even called her house to tell her that she washed her hair with barf.

Look, I was an idiot. I didn't want people to think that I had a crush, so I decided to give everyone the impression that I truly, honestly hated Madison Hartner. For no reason. Just thinking about this really makes me want to punch myself in the eyeball.

Finally, after about a week, the day came when I made her cry—something about Booger ChapStick, I forget the specifics—and the teacher gave me the elementary school equivalent of a restraining order. I quietly accepted it and didn't speak to Madison again for like five years. To this day, it remains an unsolved mystery: The Week Greg Was Filled with Unexplained Hate for Madison.

Christ.

Failed Girl Tactic #3: The Diversion. So, Mom made me go to Hebrew school until my bar mitzvah, which was a colossal pain in the ass and I don't want to talk about it. However, Hebrew school had one thing going for it: a terrific boy-girl ratio. There was just one other boy in my class, Josh Metzger, versus six girls. The problem: Only one of those girls, Leah Katzenberg, was hot. The other problem: Josh Metzger was sort of a stud. He had long

bleached-out frizzy hair from swimming. He also was sullen and untalkative, which made me afraid of him and at the same time made him very attractive to girls. Even our teachers used to hit on him. Hebrew school teachers are all women, mostly unmarried.

Anyway, in sixth grade, it was time to throw some game at Leah Katzenberg. In order to win her over—get ready for record-setting stupidity—I decided that I would try to make her jealous. Specifically, by flirting with Rachel Kushner, an average-looking girl with big teeth and hair even frizzier than Josh Metzger's. Rachel Kushner was also not especially exciting to talk to, because she talked really slowly and never seemed to have anything to say.

The one thing going for her was that she thought I was the funniest guy in the entire world. I could make her laugh by doing literally anything: impressions of teachers, going cross-eyed, Dance of the Pigeon Man. This was awesome for my self-esteem. Unfortunately, it was not awesome for my chances with Leah Katzenberg, who rapidly came to think that Rachel and I were a cute couple, and one day after Hebrew school told us exactly that.

Suddenly, I had a girlfriend. And it was not the girlfriend I wanted.

In the words of Nizar, the surliest and least-English-speaking of Benson's ESL kids, "Fuck dick shit ass."

The next day, I informed Rachel over the phone that I wanted to be Just Friends.

"That's fine," she said.

"Great," I said.

"Do you want to come over?" she asked.

"Uh," I said. "My foot is stuck in the toaster." It was idiotic, but needless to say, this got a huge laugh from her.

"Seriously, do you want to come over," she asked again, after literally thirty seconds of helpless giggling.

"I have to sort out this toaster thing first," I said. Then, knowing that there was no going forward with that conversation, I hung up.

This joke went on for days, then weeks. Sometimes when she called, I said I was glued to the fridge; other times I had accidentally welded myself to a police car. I started branching out to animals: "I have to fight some angry tigers," or "I'm digesting an entire wombat right now." It didn't even make any sense. And eventually, Rachel stopped thinking this was so funny. "Greg, seriously," she started saying. "Greg, if you don't want to hang out, just *tell* me." But I wasn't able to tell her for some reason. I would have felt too mean. The stupid part was, what I was doing was way *more* mean. But I didn't realize this at the time.

I just punched my own eyeball.

Hebrew school became incredibly awkward. Rachel stopped wanting to talk to me, but this didn't help things with Leah at all. I mean, obviously. She thought I was a huge jerk. Actually, I may have helped convince her that *all* boys were jerks, because she became a lesbian not long after the whole Rachel fiasco.

Failed Girl Tactic #4: The Boob Compliment. In seventh grade, Mara LaBastille had a terrific pair of boobs. But it's just never a good idea to compliment a girl's boobs. I had to learn this the hard way. Also, it's somehow worse to draw attention to the

fact that there are two boobs. I don't know why this is, but it's true. "You have nice boobs." Bad. "You have two nice boobs." Worse. "Two boobs? Perfect." F minus.

Failed Girl Tactic #5: The Gentleman. Mariah Epps's family moved to Pittsburgh in eighth grade. When she was introduced to us on the first day of school, I was so fired up. She was cute, she seemed smart, and best of all, she was completely unaware of my history of dickhead behavior around girls. I knew I had to move quickly. That night, I broke down and asked Mom what girls really wanted.

"Girls like gentlemen," she said. She was being kind of loud. "A girl likes to get *flowers* every so often." She was glaring at Dad. It was the day after her birthday or something.

So the second day of school, I wore a suit and brought an actual rose to school, which I gave to Mariah before first period.

"I would be honoured and delighted to escort you to an ice-cream parlour this week-end," I said, in a British accent.

"*Would* you," she said.

"Greg, you look like a fruit," said Will Carruthers, a nearby jock.

But it worked. Unbelievable! We actually went on a date. We met at a place in Oakland, and I bought us some ice cream, and we sat down, and I thought, from now on, this is how my life is going to be, and that kicks ass.

That's when The Talking began.

My God, that girl could talk. She could go for miles. Invariably it was about her friends back in Minnesota, whom I didn't know.

It was all she wanted to talk about. I heard hundreds of hours' worth of stories about these people, and because I was being a gentleman, I wasn't allowed to say, "This is boring," or "I already heard that one."

And so the problem became that the gentleman tactic worked *too* well. The expectations were ridiculous. I had to wear my nicest clothes to school every day, pay for stuff constantly, spend hours on the phone every night, etc. And for what? Definitely not sex. Gentlemen don't get to fool around. Not that I really knew, back then, what fooling around *was*. Plus I had to keep talking in that stupid British accent, and everyone thought I was brain-damaged.

So I had to put a stop to it. But how? It obviously wasn't an option to be honest and say, "Mariah, if spending time with you means paying lots of money and listening to you talk, then it's not worth it." I considered a campaign of freaking her out by suddenly only talking about dinosaurs, or maybe even pretending to *be* a dinosaur, but I didn't have the courage to do those, either. It was a major quandary.

Then, out of the blue, Aaron Winer saved the day. He took her to some movie and made out with her in the back row. The next day at school, *they* were boyfriend and girlfriend. Bam! Problem solved. I pretended to be bitter about this, but in fact I was so relieved that I started laughing hysterically in history class and had to be excused to go to the nurse.

And that was that. During high school I didn't even bother with girls or girl tactics. Frankly, the Mariah thing completely cured me of wanting to have a girlfriend. If it was going to be like that, then screw it.

Chapter 4

WHERE ARE THEY NOW?

Cameron "Cammie" Marshall is now captain of the Math League. She still has a Hello Kitty backpack, which might not be ironic. She is definitely not the hottest girl in her class anymore, although I think that does not really bother her all that much.

Madison Hartner is smokin' hot and probably dates one of the Pittsburgh Steelers or something.

Leah Katzenberg has a shaved head and a bunch of metal embedded in various parts of her face, and four out of five Benson English teachers have given up trying to make her read books written by men.

Mara LaBastille and her two equally phenomenal boobs went to a different high school.

Mariah Epps is a theater girl now. She has a posse of 100 percent gay male sidekicks, including Justin Howell, and holy shit, do they do a lot of talking.

Rachel Kushner got acute myelogenous leukemia our senior year.

Chapter 5

THE DYING GIRL

I found out about Rachel's leukemia pretty much as soon as I got home.

So, just to repeat, the first day of senior year had been, if not awesome, then unexpectedly non-horrible. Everyone, from wealthy designer-nosed Olivia Ryan to Nizar the Surly Syrian, thought I was OK, and no one was actively plotting my downfall. This was unprecedented. Plus, in general things were a lot less stressful, now that there weren't upperclassmen who could squirt mustard packets at my head or backpack. That is what being a senior is all about. My teachers were talking a lot of trash about how hard class was going to be, but by senior year, you realize that all teachers say that every year, and they are always lying.

My life had reached its highest point. I had no way of knowing that as soon as Mom walked in, the prime of my life was over. It had lasted about eight hours.

INT. MY BEDROOM — DAY

GREG is sitting on his bed. He has just gotten home from school and is trying to read *A Tale of Two Cities* for class, but it is difficult for him to maintain focus, because inside his pants he has AN INEXPLICABLE BONER. An image of some BOOBS on GREG'S LAPTOP, open nearby, is not helping things. There is a KNOCK at the door.

> MOM
> *offscreen*
> Greg? Honey? Can I come in and talk to you?

> GREG
> *quietly*
> Fuck fuck fuck

> MOM
> *entering room as GREG*
> *conspicuously shuts his computer*
> Honey, how are you doing.

MOM squats down on the floor in front of the bed with her arms folded. Her eyebrows are scrunched, she has a crease in her

forehead, and she is staring Greg in
the eyes without blinking. These are all
reliable signs that she is about to ask
Greg to do SOMETHING ANNOYING.

GREG'S INEXPLICABLE BONER is in full retreat.

                    MOM
                again
          Honey? Are you doing OK?

                    GREG
          What?

                    MOM
            after a long silence
          I have some really sad news for
          you, honey. I'm so sorry.

CLOSE-UP of Greg's confused face as
he considers what this news might be.
DAD isn't home. Maybe the university
fired him? For weirdness? Can you get
fired for weirdness? Or maybe all along
Dad has led a secret double life as a
CRIMINAL MASTERMIND? And now he's been
discovered, and the family has to flee to
an undisclosed ISLAND in the Caribbean?

Where they will live in a little hut with
a rusty tin roof and AN ACTUAL GOAT? And
will there be LOCAL GIRLS with coconut
halves on their boobs and skirts made
of foliage? Or is that Hawaii? Greg is
mistakenly thinking of Hawaii.

                    GREG
      OK.

                    MOM
      I just got off the phone with
      Denise Kushner. Rachel's mom?
      Do you know Denise?

                    GREG
      Not really.

                    MOM
      But you're friends with Rachel.

                    GREG
      Sort of.

                    MOM
      You two had kind of a thing,
      right? She was your girlfriend?

                GREG
        feeling uneasy
That was like six years ago.

                MOM
Honey, Rachel has been diagnosed with
leukemia. Denise just found out.

                GREG
Oh.
        after a short silence, stupidly
Is that serious?

                MOM
        now starting to cry a little bit
Oh, honey. They don't know.
They're doing tests, and they're
gonna do all they can. But they just
don't know.
        leaning forward
Sweetie, I'm so sorry about this.
It's really not fair. It's not *fair.*

                GREG
        sounding even more like an idiot
Uh . . . it sucks.

                    MOM
You're right. You're absolutely
right. It *does* suck.
          passionately, and also
          bizarrely, because parents don't
          say that things suck
It *does* suck. It really, really
sucks.

                    GREG
          still struggling to find
          something appropriate to say,
          and failing
This, uh, just sucks . . . really bad.
          maybe if he keeps talking, he
          will say something that is not
          stupid?
It sucks so hard.
          Jesus.
Man.

                    MOM
          breaking down
It *sucks.* You're *right. It just*
really sucks so hard. Greg. Oh
my poor baby. It sucks so very much.

GREG, feeling just insanely awkward, gets
off the bed and on the floor and tries to
hug his MOM, who is rolling back and forth
on the balls of her feet, crying. They
SQUAT-HUG for a while.

CLOSE-UP of Greg's confused and kind of
blank face; obviously he's upset, but
actually the really upsetting thing is
that he's not as sad as his mom — not
even close — and he feels guilty and
sort of resentful about this. Does Mom
even know Rachel that well? No. Why is
Mom FREAKING OUT SO MUCH about this?
Although, at the same time, why isn't
Greg freaking out more? Is Greg a bad
person for not needing to cry about this?
Greg has a premonition that this is
going to turn into some REALLY ANNOYING,
TIME-CONSUMING THING.

                    MOM
              finally crying less
          Sweetie, Rachel is going to
          need her friends now more than
          ever.

                    GREG

uhhh

                    MOM
              again, forcefully
Now *more* than ever. I know it's
hard, but you don't have a
choice. It's a *mitzvah*.

"Mitzvah" is Hebrew for "colossal pain in the ass."

                    GREG

umm

                    MOM
The more time you spend with
her, just, you know, the more
difference you can make in her
life.

                    GREG

Huh.

                    MOM
It *sucks*. But you have to be
strong. You have to be a *good
friend.*

It definitely sucked. What the hell was I supposed to do? How would it make things better if I were to call up and finally offer to hang out? What would I even say? "Hey, I heard you got leukemia. Sounds like you need an emergency prescription . . . for Greg-acil." I didn't know, for starters, what leukemia *was*. I reopened my computer.

That was when, for a second or two, Mom and I were looking at boobs.

                    MOM
                disgusted
        Ugh, Greg.

                    GREG
        How did those get there?!

                    MOM
        Let me ask you — do you actually
        like looking at those? They look so
        fake.

                    GREG
        You know what this is? They, uh,
        have these new pop-up ads on
        Facebook, and they're basically just
        porn — they just appear randomly
        sometimes —

> MOM
>
> Real breasts do not look like water
> balloons.

> GREG
>
> It's an ad.

> MOM
>
> Greg, I'm not stupid.

So it turns out leukemia is cancer of the blood cells. It's the most common kind of cancer that teenagers get, although the specific kind Rachel had—acute myelogenous leukemia—is not the normal kind for teens. "Acute" means that the leukemia basically came out of nowhere and is growing really quickly, and "myelogenous" has to do with bone marrow. Essentially, Rachel's blood and bone marrow were being invaded by aggressive, fast-moving cancer cells. I was picturing her in my mind, with her big teeth and frizzy hair, under this invisible microscopic attack, with all these screwed-up things floating around in her veins. Now I actually was getting really upset. But instead of crying, I sort of wanted to throw up.

> GREG
>
> Does everyone know about this?

> MOM
>
> I think Rachel's family is keeping
> it pretty secret, for now.

                    GREG
            alarmed
So am I not supposed to know
about it?

                    MOM
            acting a little weird
No, honey. It's fine if you know
about it.

                    GREG
But why?

                    MOM
Well, I was talking to Denise.
And, you know, we decided that
you were someone who could make
Rachel feel better.
            starting to nag
Rachel can really use a friend,
honey.

                    GREG
OK.

                    MOM
She can really use someone to
make her laugh.

                    GREG

OK OK.

                    MOM

And I just think, if you spend
some time —

                    GREG

OK OK *Jesus Christ.*

Mom gives Greg a sad and knowing look.

                    MOM

It's OK to be upset.

Chapter 6

PHONE SEX

I sat there, paralyzed by the problem of what to say. What can you possibly say to a dying person? Who might not even know that you know that they're dying? I made a list of opening lines, and none of them seemed like they would be any good.

Opening line:

Hey, this is Greg. You want to hang out?

Probable response:

Rachel: Why do you want to hang out with me all of a sudden?

Greg: Because we don't have that much time left, to hang out.

Rachel: So, you just want to hang out with me because I'm dying.

Greg: I just want to get in some Rachel time! You know! While I still can.

Rachel: This is probably the most insensitive conversation I have ever had with anyone.

Greg: Do-over time.

Opening line:

Hey, this is Greg. I heard about your leukemia, and I'm calling to make you feel better.

Probable response:

Rachel: Why would you calling make me feel better?

Greg: Because! Uh. I dunno!

Rachel: You're just reminding me of all those times you never wanted to hang out with me.

Greg: Hoo boy.

Rachel: Right now, you're screwing up my last days of existence. That's what you're doing.

Greg:

Rachel: I have just a few more days on this earth, and you're smearing your barf on those days.

Greg: Fuck, let me try this again.

Opening line:

Hey, this is Greg. You, me, and some pasta makes three.

Probable response:

Rachel: Huh?

Greg: I'm taking you out on a *date.* Greg style.

Rachel: What?

Greg: Listen to me. Our remaining days with each other are few, and precious. Let's make up for lost time. Let's be together.

Rachel: Oh my God, that's so romantic.

Greg:

Greg: Damn it.

There just wasn't a good way to do it. Mom was asking me to resume a friendship that had no honest foundation and ended on screamingly awkward terms. How do you do that? You can't.

"Hello? Who is this?" said Rachel's mom over the phone. She sounded aggressive and was kind of barking like a dog. This was standard behavior for Mrs. Kushner.

"Uh, hi, this is Greg," I said. Then for some reason, instead of asking for Rachel's number, I said, "How are you doing?"

"Gre-e-e-eg," oozed Mrs. Kushner. "I'm fi-i-i-ine." Boom. In an instant, her tone had changed completely. This was a side of her I had never seen, nor had I ever hoped to see it.

"That's great," I said.

"Greg, how are you-u-u-u." She was now using a voice that women usually reserve for cats.

"Uh, good," I said.

"And how is schoo-o-o-ool."

"Just trying to get it over with," I said, then immediately realized what a colossally stupid thing that was to say to someone whose daughter had cancer, and I almost hung up. But then she said: "Greg, you're so funny. You've always been such a funny kid."

It sounded like she meant it, but she wasn't laughing at all. This was getting even weirder than I had feared.

"I was calling to maybe get Rachel's number," I said.

"She. Would. *Love.* To hear from you."

"Yup," I agreed.

"She's in her room right now, just waiting around."

I had no idea what to make of that sentence. In her room,

just waiting around. Waiting for me? Or for death? My God, that's bleak. I tried to put a positive spin on it.

"Livin' it up," I said.

This was the second brain-punchingly insensitive thing I had said in about thirty seconds, and again I considered closing my cell phone and eating it.

But: "Greg, you have such a good *sense of humor*," Mrs. Kushner informed me. "Never let them take that away from you, all right? Always keep your sense of humor."

"'Them'?" I said, alarmed.

"People," Mrs. Kushner said. "The whole world."

"Huh," I said.

"The world tries to just beat you down, Greg," announced Mrs. Kushner. "They just want to crush the life out of you." I had no response to this, and then she said, "I don't even know what I'm *saying*."

Mrs. Kushner had lost it. It was time to ride the wave or drown in a sea of crazy.

"Hallelujah," I said. "Preach."

"Preach," she crowed. She actually cackled. "Greg!"

"Mrs. Kushner!"

"You can call me Denise," she said, terrifyingly.

"Awesome," I said.

"Here's Rachel's number," said Denise, and gave it to me, and thank God, that was that. It almost made me relieved to talk to my sort-of-kinda-not-really ex-girlfriend about her imminent death.

"Hi, this is Rachel."

"Hey, this is Greg."

"Hi."

"Yo."

". . ."

"I called the doctor and he said you needed a prescription of Greg-acil."

"What's that."

"That's me."

"Oh."

"Uh, in convenient gel-tab form."

"Oh."

"Yeahhhh."

"So I guess you heard that I'm sick."

"Yeahhhh."

"Did my mom tell you?"

"Uh, my mom told me."

"Oh."

"So, uh."

"What?"

"What?"

"What were you going to say?"

"Uhhh."

"Greg, what?"

"Well, I was calling . . . to see . . . if you wanted to hang out."

"Right now?"

"Uh, sure."

"No thanks."

"Uh . . . you don't want to hang out?"

"No, thanks anyway."

"Well, maybe later then."

"Maybe later."

"OK, uh . . . bye."

"Bye."

I hung up feeling like the biggest douchebag in the world. Somehow the conversation was 100 percent what I was expecting, yet I still managed to be blindsided by it. By the way, this kind of awkward fiasco was always what happened when Mom tried to get involved in my social life. Let me point out here that it's acceptable for moms to try to run their kids' social lives when the kids are in kindergarten or whatever. But I have a mom who didn't stop scheduling play dates for me until I reached the ninth grade. The worst part of that was that the only other twelve and thirteen-year-olds whose moms scheduled their play dates were kids with mild to serious developmental disorders. I'm not going to go into detail about that, but let's just say that it was emotionally scarring and is possibly a reason I spend so much time freaking out and pretending to be dead.

Anyway. What you're seeing here is just part of a larger pattern of Mom-Greg Life Interference. She was without a doubt the single biggest obstacle between me and the social life that I was trying to describe before: a social life without friends, enemies, or awkwardness.

I guess I should introduce my family. Please forgive me if this sucks.

Chapter 7

THE GAINES FAMILY: A SUMMARY

Again, let's try and get this over with as quickly as possible.

Dr. Victor Gaines: That would be my dad, a professor of classics at Carnegie Mellon University. No human being is weirder than Victor Quincy Gaines, PhD. My theory on Dad is that he was a party animal in the '80s, and drugs and alcohol have partially unraveled the wiring of his brain. One of his favorite things to do is sit in a rocking chair in the living room, rock back and forth, and stare at the wall. Around the house he usually wears a muumuu, which is essentially a blanket with holes cut in it, and he talks to the cat, Cat Stevens, as if he were a real human being.

It's hard not to be envious of Dad. He teaches at most two classes per semester, usually one, and that seems to occupy a very small percentage of his week. Sometimes they give him the entire year off to write a book. Dad has very little patience for most of the other professors he works with. He thinks they whine too much. Dad spends a lot of his time at specialty food shops on the Strip, chatting with the owners and buying obscure animal products that no one else in the family will eat, like yak tripe and ostrich sausage and dried cuttlefish.

Every two years, Dad grows a beard, and it makes him look like a member of the Taliban.

Marla Gaines: And that's my mom, Marla, the ex-hippie. Mom led a very interesting life before she married Dad, but the details are carefully guarded. We know that she lived in Israel at some point, and we suspect that she may have had a boyfriend in the Saudi royal family, which would have been sort of a big deal, because she is Jewish. In fact, Marla Weissman Gaines is *very* Jewish. She is the executive director of Ahavat Ha'Emet, a nonprofit that sends Jewish teenagers to Israel to work on a kibbutz and lose their virginity. I should point out that the virginity-losing part is not technically in the mission statement of Ahavat Ha'Emet. I'm just saying, you do not leave Israel without getting laid. You could have an eight-inch-thick titanium diaper bolted to your pelvis, and you would still somehow get laid. It should be their official tourism slogan: **Israel. Where Virginity Goes to Die.™**

Israelis get it on.

Anyway, my mom is a very loving woman, and she lets Dad do whatever the hell he wants, but she is also very opinionated and strong-willed, especially when it comes to Matters of Right and Wrong, and when she decides that something is the Right Thing to Do, that thing gets done. No ifs, ands, or buts. For better or worse. Whether we like it or not. This characteristic, in moms, is a colossal pain in the ass, and it basically ruined my life as I knew it, as well as Earl's. Thanks a lot, Mom.

Gretchen Gaines: Gretchen is my older younger sister. She's fourteen, which means that any kind of normal interaction with her is doomed to failure. We used to be pretty good friends, but fourteen-year-old girls are psychotic. Her main interests are yelling at Mom and not eating whatever is for dinner.

Grace Gaines: Grace is my younger younger sister. She's six. Gretchen and I are pretty sure Grace was an accident. Incidentally, you may have noticed that all of our names begin with *GR* and are not at all Jewish-sounding. One night Mom had a little too much wine at dinner and confided to us all that, before we were born, and after she realized her children would have Dad's also-not-Jewish last name, she decided she wanted all of us to be "surprise Jews." Meaning, Jews with sneaky Anglo-Saxon names. I know, it makes no sense. I guess it shows that a vulnerability to brain fungus runs in the family.

Anyway, Grace aspires to be a writer and a princess, and like Dad, she treats Cat Stevens as though he is a human being.

Cat Stevens Gaines: Cat Stevens was awesome, once—he used to do things like stand up on his back paws and hiss whenever you entered the room, or run up to you in the hallway and wrap his arms around your shin and start biting you—but now he's old and slow. You can still get him to bite you, but you have to grab his tummy and jiggle it. Technically, he's my cat; I was the one who named him. I came up with the name when I was seven, having recently learned about Cat Stevens's existence from National Public Radio, which of course is the only radio station that gets any burn in the Gaines house. It seemed like an obvious name for a cat at the time.

Only years later did I realize that Cat Stevens, the musician, is totally beat.

I cannot emphasize this enough: Dad has a *strong* affinity for Cat Stevens (the cat). In addition to sharing long-winded philosophical meditations with him, sometimes Dad plays Cat Stevens like a drum, which is a thing that Cat Stevens loves. Cat Stevens is also the only other member of the family who enjoys eating the meats that Dad brings home from the Strip, although sometimes he expresses his enjoyment by barfing.

Gamma-Gamma Gaines: Dad's mom lives in Boston and comes to visit occasionally. As with Cat Stevens, I named her when I was a toddler, and now I don't get a do-over, and me and my sisters all have to call her Gamma-Gamma. It's embarrassing. I guess we all make mistakes when we're young.

Chapter 8

PHONE SEX II

I found out about Rachel's leukemia on a Tuesday. Wednesday, I tried calling her again after more nagging from Mom, and again she didn't want to hang out. Thursday, she hung up as soon as I said my name.

So on Friday, I had no intention of calling whatsoever. When I got home from school, I went straight to the TV room to watch a movie. Specifically, *Alphaville* (Godard, 1965), which I was then going to re-watch later with Earl for research purposes. I realize you have no idea who Earl is still, even though we're deep into this unbearably stupid book. Earl will be introduced soon, probably after I attempt to slam a door on my own head.

Anyway, I was barely into the credits when Mom walked in and pulled one of her trademark moves. She shut off the TV, opened her mouth, and emitted a nonstop stream of words. Nothing I did could make her stop talking. This is an unstoppable move.

MOM

You do not have a choice about this,
Gregory, because you have been
presented with the opportunity to
make a very real difference in som

GREG

Mom what the hell

MOM

s rare and above all meaningful thing
that you could be doing and let me
tell you that it is not

GREG

Is this about Rachel? Because

MOM

nd I've seen you day after day
just lying around like a dead slug
and meanwhile a friend of yours

GREG

Can I just say something?

MOM

completely unacceptable, *completely*,

you've got all the time in the world,
and Rachel frankly doe

> GREG
>
> Mom stop talking can I just say
> something

> MOM
>
> f you think any of your excuses are
> more important than the happiness of
> a girl with

> GREG
>
> Holy shit. Please stop talking.

> MOM
>
> ou are going to *pick* up your phone,
> you are going to *call* Rachel, you
> are going to *arrange to spend*

> GREG
>
> Rachel won't even let me say anything!
> She just hangs up! Mom! SHE JUST HANGS UP.

> MOM
>
> n this world, bottom line, you're
> gonna have to learn to give, because
> *you've* been given everythi

GREG

UUUUUUUUURRRRRRRRRRGGGG

MOM

think you can "urrrg" your way out
of this one, buster, you can think
again, nuh-uh, no way, you

There was nothing to be done. I had to call Rachel.
You can't fight Mom's unstoppable move. It's probably how
Mom got to be boss of a nonprofit: Nonprofits are all about
persuading people to do stuff by talking at them. It's like Will
Carruthers talking you into giving him your Doritos "one
time," except that the nonprofit doesn't have the additional
persuasive advantage of you worrying that later the nonprofit
is going to jump you in the locker room and whip your naked
buttocks with a towel.

So yeah, I had to call Rachel again.

"What do you want."

"Hi please don't hang up."

"I said, what do you want."

"I want to hang out with you. Come on."

". . ."

"Rachel?"

"So you ignore me in school, and then you want to hang
out after school."

Well, this was true. Rachel and I had a few classes together, including calculus, where we sat right next to each other, and yeah, I made no effort to talk to her during any of that time. But I mean, that's just what I did in school. I didn't make an effort to talk to *anyone*. No friends, no enemies. That was the whole point.

If you think I had any idea of how to say this on the phone, though, you have not really been paying attention. I am about as good of a communicator as Cat Stevens, and only a little less likely to bite you.

"No, I wasn't ignoring you."

"Yeah, you were."

"I thought you were ignoring *me*."

" . . . "

"So, yeah."

"You always *used* to ignore me, though."

"Uh."

"I always figured you just didn't want to be friends with me."

"Uhhh."

" . . . "

" . . . "

"Greg?"

"The thing is, you broke my heart."

I'm smart in some ways—pretty good vocabulary, solid at math—but I am definitely the stupidest smart person there is.

"*I* broke *your* heart."

"Well, sort of."

"How did I 'sort of' break your heart."

"Uh . . . Remember Josh?"

"Josh Metzger?"

"In Hebrew school I thought you were in love with Josh."

"Why did you think *that*?"

"I thought *everyone* in our class was in love with Josh."

"Josh was depressed all the time."

"No, he was all sullen and, uh . . . and dreamy."

"Greg, it sounds like *you're* in love with Josh."

"Harf!"

This was unexpected. It had never happened before. Rachel had made *me* laugh. I mean, what she said wasn't that funny, but I just really wasn't expecting it, which is why instead of a normal laugh I made a sound like *harf.* Anyway, that's when I knew I was in.

"You really thought I was in love with Josh."

"Yeah."

"And that broke your heart?"

"Of *course* it did."

"Well, you should've said something."

"Yeah, I was being really stupid about it."

One of my few effective conversational tactics is to throw

previous versions of myself under the bus. Twelve-year-old Greg was a jerk to you, you say? He was a jerk to *everyone*. And he had like thirty stuffed animals in his room! What a loser.

"Greg, I'm sorry."
"No! No, no, no. It's my fault."
"Well, what are you doing right now?"
"Nothing," I lied.
"You can come over if you want."

Mission accomplished. I just had to call Earl.

Chapter 9

A MORE OR LESS TYPICAL CONVERSATION WITH EARL

"Hey, Earl?"

"Sup, ike."

"Ike" is a good sign. It's slang for "dude," and when Earl uses it, that means he's in a good mood, which is rare.

"Hey, Earl, I can't watch *Alphaville* today."

"Why the hell not?"

"I'm sorry, man, I have to hang out with this girl from, uh— this girl from synagogue."

"Wha-a-at."

"She's—"

"Are you gonna eat her pussy?"

Earl can be sort of profane sometimes. He's actually mellowed out a lot since his middle school days, believe it or not. Back in middle school he would have asked this in a much more violent and horrible way.

"Yeah, Earl, I'm going to eat her pussy."

"Heh."

"Yeah."

"Do you even know *how* to eat pussy?"

"Uh, not really."

"Papa Gaines never sat you down, said, Son, one day you're gonna have to eat the pussy."

"No. But he did teach me how to eat a butthole."

When Earl is in full-on Gross-Out Mode, you have to play along or you'll feel stupid.

"God bless that man."

"Yup."

"*I* would teach you some pussy-eating technique, but it's a little complicated."

"That's a shame."

"I would need some diagrams and whatnot."

"Well, tonight maybe you can draw some up."

"Son, I don't have time for that. I got like twenty pussies over here that I need to eat."

"Is that right."

"I'm on pussy deadline."

"You've got twenty vaginas, all lined up in a row."

"Aw, what the hell. What the *hell*. No one's talkin bout *vaginas*. Greg, what the hell is wrong with you. Man, that's nasty."

Earl likes to mix it up sometimes by pretending that you're

being gross and he is not, when he's clearly being much grosser. This is a classic humor move that he has perfected over the years.

"Oh, sorry."

"Man, you're sick. You're perverted."

"Yeah, that was really out of line."

"I'm talkin bout *pussy.* I got a little honey mustard over here, a little Heinz 57, and a whole lotta pussy."

"Yeah, that's not gross. What I said was gross, but not what you just said."

"Got some Grey Poupon up in this. Got some *Hellmann's.*"

Gross-Out Mode can last indefinitely and sometimes you just have to change the subject without warning if you actually have a message to convey.

"So yeah, sorry I can't watch Godard tonight."

"So you wanna watch it tomorrow?"

"Yeah, let's do it tomorrow."

"After school. Try to get some of them little steak tips."

"OK, but I don't think Mom is making beef tips tonight."

"*Steak. Tips.* Give Ma and Pa Gaines some love for me, ike."

Earl and I are friends. Sort of. Actually, Earl and I are more like coworkers.

The first thing to know about Earl Jackson is that if you mention his height, he will windmill-kick you in the head. Short people are often extremely athletic. Earl is technically the size of

a ten-year-old, but he can kick any object within seven feet of the ground. Additionally, Earl's default mood is Pissed, and his backup default mood is Mega-Pissed.

It's not just that he's short, either. He *looks* really young. He has a sort of round bug-eyed Yoda-esque face that makes girls go all motherly and start cooing. Grown-ups don't really take him seriously, especially teachers. They have trouble talking to him as though he's a normal human being. They bend down way too far and speak in this ridiculous up-and-down singsong: "*Hel*-lo *Ear*-rul!" It's like he gives off an invisible force field that makes people stupid.

The worst part is that his whole family is taller than him—all of his brothers and half brothers, his stepsisters, his cousins, his aunts and uncles, his stepdad, even his mom. It's not really fair. At family barbecues, he gets his head playfully rubbed by someone about every ninety seconds, and it's not always someone older than him, either. He is constantly being pushed out of the way by people who don't even realize they're pushing him out of the way. He can't wander out into the open; if he does, his brothers take turns running up and leapfrogging over his head. You would be perpetually angry at the world, too, if this was your life.

However, from some perspectives, Earl's home life is awesome. He lives basically unsupervised with two brothers, three half brothers, and a dog in a huge house a few blocks above Penn Avenue, and they play video games and eat Domino's pizza pretty much all of the time. His mom lives in the house, too, but she usually restricts herself to the third floor. What she does up there is rarely discussed—especially with Earl around—but

I can tell you that it involves Bacardi Silver mojitos and chat rooms. Meanwhile, downstairs it's six guys in a house, living it up. Nonstop party! What problems could there possibly be?

Problem 1. Well, there is the troublesome matter of the house's finances. There are no dads in the house—Earl's dad is in Texas or something, and the half brothers' dad is in prison—and Earl's mom provides little in the way of income. Two of the half brothers, the twins, Maxwell and Felix, are in one of Homewood's enterprising gangs—Tha Frankstown Murda Cru—and provide some of the family's financial support by dealing drugs. Earl himself has done most of the major drugs, although these days, he smokes only cigarettes. So, there's some drug dealing and gang activity in the house, which probably counts as a problem.

Problems 2 and 3. I guess I should also note that there's a bit of a noise problem—video games, music, yelling—and a smell problem as well. There's generally garbage lying around, often with little pools of garbage juice underneath, and the brothers don't really do that much laundry. Sometimes someone will also get really drunk and throw up on the floor, and that can take days to clean up, as do the frequent hills of poop created by the dog. I don't want to sound like a "pussy-ass bitch" (Felix's words), but this is surely less than ideal, as living situations go.

Problem 4. It's also not an incredibly scholarly environment. Earl is the only one still attending school every day; Devin and Derrick can go for weeks without showing up; all of the half

brothers have dropped out, including Brandon, who is thirteen and probably the most violent and aggressive of the bunch. (For example, he has a huge painful-looking neck tattoo that says "TRU NIGGA" next to some pictures of guns. Brandon himself owns a gun and has already managed to impregnate another human being, even though his voice hasn't dropped all the way yet. If the city of Pittsburgh gave out a Least Promising Human award, he would be on the shortlist.) Due to the noise problems mentioned above, the Jackson house is not a great place to try to read, or do homework, or do any kind of work; also, if someone finds you alone in a room with a book, sometimes this is considered sufficient grounds to whup the hell out of you.

Problems 5 through 10. The house itself is kind of falling apart—there's a big chunk of the gutters lying in the front yard, and the ceiling drips in some of the bedrooms, and usually at least one of the toilets is clogged and no one really wants to deal with it. In the winter, the heating generally conks out and everyone has to sleep in their winter coat. There's definitely a rat problem, and a cockroach problem, and it's not a good idea to drink the tap water.

The video games, however, are solid.

So Earl and I, when we hang out, usually hang out at my house instead. By now Earl is almost a member of the family: the chain-smoking vertically challenged son my parents never had. They're the only grown-ups besides Mr. McCarthy who even sort of know how to talk to him without pissing him off. Emphasis on "sort of." Their interactions with him are always kind of surreal.

INT. LIVING ROOM OF MY HOUSE — DAY

DAD is sitting in his rocking chair, contemplating the wall, as he likes to do. CAT STEVENS is asleep on the couch. Enter EARL, on his way to the front door, smacking a fresh pack of cigarettes against the palm of his hand.

>   EARL
>   How's life, Mr. Gaines.

>   DAD
>   *echoing mysteriously*
>   Life.

>   EARL
>   *patiently*
>   How's your life.

>   DAD
>   Life! Yes, life. Life is good, as I
>   was just telling Cat Stevens here.
>   How's your life?

>   EARL
>   It's goin' awright.

                    DAD
You're going out for a cigarette
break, I see.

                    EARL
Yeah. You want to come?

                    DAD
          five seconds of unexplained
          staring

                    EARL
Awright then.

                    DAD
Earl, would you agree that suffering
in life is a, a relative notion —
that for every life there is a
different baseline, an equilibrium,
below which one can be said to
suffer?

                    EARL
I guess.

                    DAD
The primary insight being that one
man's suffering is another man's joy.

                    EARL
        Sounds good, Mr. Gaines.

                    DAD
        Very well then.

                    EARL
        I'ma go smoke one of these.

                    DAD
        Godspeed, young man.

Maybe 80 percent of the interaction between Dad and Earl is along those lines. The rest is when Dad takes Earl to a specialty food place or Whole Foods and they buy something unspeakably disgusting and then eat it together. It's a weird scene and I've learned to stay away.

The Mom-Earl conversations are slightly less insane. She likes to tell him that he's "a hoot," and she's learned that it doesn't really do any good to try to get him to quit smoking, and as long as *I'm* not smoking, she'll allow it. For his part, even on days when he's mega-pissed, he tones it down when he's around her and doesn't do any of his trademark rage-expressing mannerisms, such as stomping his feet really fast and growling the consonant "ngh." He doesn't even threaten to kick anyone in the head.

So that's Earl. I've probably missed a bunch of stuff and will have to describe Earl in greater detail later, but there's no reason to believe that you'll still be reading the book at that time, so I guess I would say don't worry about it.

Chapter 10

I PUT THE "ASS" IN "CASANOVA"

On the way to Rachel's house, I realized that I had just been a colossal idiot.

"You idiot, Greg," I thought, and may also have said out loud. "Now she thinks you've been in love with her for five years."

Moron. I could picture the scene in my head: I was going to show up, ring the doorbell, and Rachel would fling open the door and embrace me, her frizzy hair bouncing, her biggish teeth grazing my cheek. Then we would have to make out, or talk about how much we loved each other. Just thinking about this was making me sweaty.

And, of course, she had cancer. What if she wanted to talk about death? That would be a disaster, right? Because I had somewhat extreme beliefs about death: There's no afterlife, and nothing happens after you die, and it's just the end of your consciousness forever. Was I going to have to lie about that? That would definitely be way too depressing, right? Was I going to have to make up some afterlife for reassurance purposes? Did it need to have those creepy naked baby angels that you see sometimes?

What if she wanted to get married? So she could have a wedding before dying? I wouldn't be allowed to say no, right? My God, what if she wanted to have sex? Would I even be able to get a boner? I was pretty sure it would be impossible for me to get a boner in those circumstances.

These were the questions running through my mind as I trudged, with growing despair, to her doorstep. But it was Denise who answered the door.

"Gre-e-e-eg," she purred, in her cat-voice. "It is so good to *see* you-u-u-u-u."

"Right back at you, Denise," I said.

"Greg, you're a riot."

"I'm illegal in twelve states."

"HA." This was a huge cackle. Then there was another one. "HA."

"I have a Surgeon General's warning tattooed on my butt."

"STOP IT. STOP. IT. HA-A-A-A." Why do I never have this effect on the girls I want to impress? Why is it only moms and homely girls? When it's just them, I can really turn it on. I don't know what it is.

"Rachel's upstairs. Can I get you a Diet Coke?"

"No thanks." I wanted to end with a bang, so I added, "Caffeine just makes me more obnoxious."

"Hang on."

This was in a completely different tone of voice. We were back to the old snappish, aggressive Mrs. Kushner. "Greg, who says you're obnoxious?"

"Oh. Uh, people, you know—"

"Listen. You tell them: They can just *shove* it."

"No, yeah. I was just saying that as a—"

"Hey. Nuh-uh. You listening to me? You tell them: They can shove it."

"They can shove it, yeah."

"The world needs more guys like you. *Not* less."

Now I was getting alarmed. Was there a campaign to get rid of guys like me? Because that campaign would probably *start* with me.

"Yes ma'am."

"Rachel's upstairs."

I went upstairs.

Rachel's room had no IV stands or heart-rate monitors like I was expecting. Actually, I had been picturing her room as a hospital room, with like a full-time nurse hanging out in there. Instead, I can sum up Rachel's bedroom in two words: pillows; posters. Her bed had at least fifteen pillows on it, and the walls were 100 percent posters and magazine cutouts. There was a lot of Hugh Jackman and Daniel Craig, especially without their shirts. If you were to show me this room and make me guess who lived in it, my answer would be: a fifteen-headed alien who stalks male human celebrities.

But instead of an alien, it was Rachel, standing sort of uncomfortably near the door.

"Rachel-l-l-l," I said.

"Hello," she said.

We stood there, motionless. How the hell were we supposed

to greet each other? I took a step forward with my arms out, for hugging purposes, but that just made me feel like a zombie. She took a step backward, frightened. At that point I had to go with it.

"I am the Zombie Hug Monster," I said, lurching forward.

"Greg, I'm afraid of zombies."

"You should not fear the Zombie Hug Monster. The Zombie Hug Monster does not want to eat your brains."

"Greg, *stop it.*"

"OK."

"What are you doing."

"Uh, I was going for a fist pound."

I *was* going for a fist pound.

"No thanks."

Just to summarize: I lurched into Rachel's room like a zombie, freaking her out, then went for a fist pound. It is impossible to be less smooth than Greg S. Gaines.

"I like your room."

"Thanks."

"How many pillows is that?"

"I don't know."

"I wish I had that many pillows."

"Why don't you ask your parents for some?"

"They wouldn't like that."

I have no idea why I said that.

"Why not?"

"Uh."

"They're *pillows.*"

"Yeah, they'd be suspicious or something."

"That you'd sleep all the time?"

"No, uh . . . They'd probably think I was just going to masturbate all over them."

I would like to point out that I conducted the above conversation 100 percent on autopilot.

Rachel was silent; her mouth was hanging open and her eyes were kind of bugging out.

Eventually, she said: "That is *disgusting.*" But she was also making snorting noises. I remembered the snort from Hebrew school; it indicated that there were some huge laughs on the way.

"That's my parents," I said. "They're gross."

"They won't get you pillows [snort] because they think you're going to [snort snort], they think you're going to masturb[SNORTsnortsnortsnort]."

"Yeah, they have really gross ideas about me."

Now Rachel couldn't even talk. She had completely lost control. She was laughing and snorting so hard that I was a little worried about her rupturing her spleen or something. Nonetheless, a fun thing to do when Rachel is in the throes of a mega-laugh is to see how long you can keep it going.

- "I mean, it's also their fault for getting sexy pillows."
- "We had this one pillow in the house, they had to burn it, because that thing just got me so aroused."

- "That was the sexiest pillow, I just, I just wanted to make love to it all night, until the break of dawn."
- "I used to call that pillow the dirtiest names. I used to say, 'You slutty pillow, you're such a dirty slut, stop *toying with my emotions.*'"
- "The pillow's name was Francesca."
- "Then one day I came home from school and caught that pillow having oral sex with this table from across the street, and—OK, OK. I'll stop."

Rachel was begging me to stop. I shut up and let her calm down. I had forgotten how hard she could laugh. It took her a while to catch her breath.

"Oh—ohhh—*ow*—oohh."

The Greg S. Gaines Three-Step Method of Seduction
1. Lurch into girl's bedroom pretending to be a zombie.
2. Go for a fist pound.
3. Suggest that you habitually masturbate all over pillows.

"Do I have to keep you away from *my* pillows?" she asked, still having involuntary laugh-snort-spasms.

"No. Are you serious? Those pillows are all dudes."

Two words: mucus explosion. However, the problem with mega-laughs is that they're hard to follow up. Sooner or later you're all laughed out, and there's this big silence. Then what do you do?

"So I guess you really like films."

"They're OK."

"I mean, you have all these actors all over your room."

"Huh?"

"Hugh Jackman, Hugh Jackman, Daniel Craig, Hugh Jackman, Ryan Reynolds, Daniel Craig, Brad Pitt."

"It's not really about the movies."

"Oh."

She was sitting at her desk and I was sitting on her bed. It was way too soft of a bed. I had sunk into it to an uncomfortable degree.

"I like movies," said Rachel, sort of apologetically. "But a movie doesn't have to be good if it has Hugh Jackman."

Fortunately and unfortunately, at that moment I got a text from Earl.

yo pa gaines drove me to whole foods so if you need some funky vlasic pickle relish for that pussy just hollerrr

This was fortunate because it changed the subject from movies, and it was going to be difficult to discuss movies with Rachel without mentioning my filmmaking career, which for obvious reasons I did not want to mention. But it was unfortunate in that it made me do a sort of snarfing laugh and then Rachel wanted to know what had happened.

"Who was that from?"

"Uh, that was from Earl."

"Oh."

"You know Earl? Earl Jackson, from high school?"

"I don't think so."

How the hell was I even supposed to introduce Earl.

"Uh, Earl and I send each other disgusting texts sometimes."

"Oh."

"That's basically our entire friendship."

"What does that one say?"

I considered sharing it with her. Then I decided that that would bring about the apocalypse.

"I can't show it to you. It is way too disgusting."

This was a tactical error, because a more annoying girl might have said, "Greg, now you *have* to show it to me," and let's face it: Most girls are annoying. I mean, most *humans* are annoying, so it's not specific to girls. Also, I don't really mean "annoying." I guess I mean that most humans like to try to fuck up your plans.

But one thing you could say about Rachel was this: She wasn't constantly trying to fuck up your plans.

"That's fine. You don't have to show it to me."

"You really don't want to see it."

"I don't need to see it."

"All you need to know is that it's about the combination of food and sex. Like, oral sex."

"Greg, why are you telling me about it."

"Just so you can know for sure that it's something you don't want to know about."

"Why is Earl combining food and oral sex?"

"Because he's a psychopath."

"Oh."

"He's just completely insane. If you looked into his brain for even one second you would probably go blind."

"He sounds like a pretty weird friend."

"Yeah."

"How did you guys end up being friends?"

There was no good way to answer this seemingly innocuous question.

"I mean, *I'm* also pretty weird."

This actually got Rachel to do a little aftershock snort.

"I guess the pillow thing is weird."

Earl and I *are* both pretty weird. And maybe that is why we're friends. But probably you deserve more of an explanation than that.

Also, what the hell does "weird" even mean? I've just written it like five times and all of a sudden I'm staring at it and it doesn't even mean anything anymore. I just murdered the word "weird." Now it's just a bunch of letters. It's like there's all these dead bodies all over the page now.

I'm sort of close to having a freak-out about this. I have to go eat some snacks or leftovers or something.

OK, I'm back.

Although, let's just do a new chapter, because this chapter got really fucked up somehow and I'm afraid of what will happen if I continue with it.

Chapter 11

I, THE WRATH OF GOD, WILL MARRY MY OWN DAUGHTER, AND TOGETHER WE SHALL START THE PUREST DYNASTY THE WORLD HAS EVER SEEN

Earl and I come from very different worlds, obviously. And it's definitely insane that we even became friends in the first place. In some ways our friendship makes no sense at all. I guess I'll just give you the backstory of it and let you draw your own conclusions. Then we can make our triumphant return to Cancerland.

Cancerland is not nearly as popular of a board game as Candyland.

Some observers would conclude that our friendship is a triumph of Pittsburgh's public school system, but I would tell you that instead it's a testament to the power of video games. Mom has never allowed video games in the house, except for the educational kind, like Math Blaster, and that wasn't so much to teach us math as to teach us that video games sucked. However, my first encounter with Earl left no doubt that video games were, in fact, awesome.

It was the second or third week of kindergarten. So far I had made it without having to interact with any of the other kindergarteners—that was my primary objective, because all of

the other kindergarteners seemed to be evil, or boring, or both—but one day Miss Szczerbiak had us sit in groups and decorate cardboard boxes. It was me, Earl, and two girls whose names I forget. All the girls wanted to do was cover the box in glitter, but Earl and I recognized that this would look terrible.

"Let's make a gun out of it," said Earl.

I thought this was awesome.

"The laser gun from GoldenEye," added Earl.

I had no idea what that meant.

"GoldenEye for N64," explained Earl. "My brothers got an N64 and *they* let me play it whenever I want."

"I have Math Blaster on my computer at home," I said.

"I never heard of Math Blaster," said Earl dismissively.

"You have to do math problems and then it lets you shoot pieces of garbage," I said. Then, realizing how pathetic this sounded, I shut up. I was hoping that somehow Earl hadn't heard. But he had, and he looked at me with both pity and scorn.

"In GoldenEye you don't have to do no math, and you get to shoot *people*," said Earl triumphantly, and that settled it. As the girls dutifully coated the box in glitter and had a discussion about pixies or domesticity or whatever, Earl and I sat at the other end of the table and Earl told me the entire plot of GoldenEye three times. Pretty soon it was agreed that after school, I was going to Earl's house. As fate would have it, it was Dad picking me up from school that day, and he saw nothing wrong with sending his kid off to Homewood with some other kid he had never met before, plus that kid's two rambunctious brothers, one of whom was repeatedly promising to shoot everyone else to death.

Earl had lied in at least one respect: The brothers, in fact, did *not* let Earl play N64 whenever he wanted to. When we got to the Jackson house, Devin (the oldest) announced that he had to complete a mission before we did anything else.

So we sat on the floor, in the glow of the screen, and it was the best thing I had ever experienced. We were in the presence of a master. We watched in rapturous happiness as Devin steered a tank through the streets of St. Petersburg, laying waste to everything in his path. We did not make a fuss when Devin told us he was going to do a second mission. We marveled as he snuck around a battleship, quietly murdering dozens of people.

"Now y'all can play me," Devin said, switching to the multi-player option. I picked up a controller. It had more knobs and buttons than I could reach with all of my fingers, so I tried getting a foot involved. That did not particularly work out. Earl tried to explain how it worked, but soon gave up. It was clear that he himself was not much of an expert. For twenty minutes, we jogged around a snowy Siberian missile base, threw grenades at random into the forest, got trapped against walls because we didn't know how to turn around, and were slaughtered by Devin, who chose a new and exciting weapon each time: the assault rifle, the shotgun, the laser pistol. Earl's other brother Derrick ignored me and Earl completely, choosing to do battle with the master alone. It was a losing effort. Taunting us mercilessly and without cease, Devin painted the tundra red with our blood.

"Y'all both suck donkey dick," said Devin at the end. "Now get the hell out of here."

A friendship had been born. Earl was definitely the leader,

and I was the sidekick. Even when we weren't playing video games, I deferred to him, because he was far worldlier than me. He knew where the alcohol was in his kitchen, for example. I was worried we were going to have to try some, but fortunately that wasn't part of the plan. "Alcohol gimme a damn headache," he explained at some point.

Back then, the Jackson household was more in control. Earl's stepdad was still living there, and his half brothers were toddlers, and Earl's mom hadn't begun her third-floor exile yet. I got to see the collapse of Earl's house firsthand. That's not really the story I want to tell, so I won't go into detail, but basically Earl's stepdad moved out and then got sent to jail, Earl's mom went through a few boyfriends, she started drinking a lot, and then around the time when the youngest half brothers got to kindergarten, she pretty much gave up on everything and started hanging out in chat rooms 24/7. I saw a lot of this as it was happening, but I was really only able to put the story together after the fact. And even now I don't have a great sense of it. It was a hard place for me to understand.

Anyway. As things got worse over the years, we spent less time at his house and eventually starting hanging out at mine. But at my house, it wasn't clear what there was to do. We tried playing board games, and that sucked. We busted out some G.I. Joes, but playing with them was so much lamer than video games that we felt like we were going insane. We ran around the house with water guns hunting Cat Stevens, but Dad made us stop after we broke some stuff. Finally, we went on a desperate search through the house one Sunday afternoon for anything even remotely close to video games, and that was how Earl found Dad's DVD collection.

For some reason I had never really been interested in Dad's DVDs. The only movies I had ever even thought to watch were animated and G-rated. These other non-animated movies had struck me as something for grown-ups. Basically, I just kind of assumed they were boring. And probably if I tried to watch them on my own they would have bored the hell out of me.

But Earl found them, and started freaking out and going all bug-eyed and saying, "Yeah, this is the shit," and something clicked in my head and I saw them completely differently.

He was especially excited about *Aguirre, the Wrath of God.* "Look at this crazy dude," he yelled, pointing at Klaus Kinski, who on the cover is wearing a Viking helmet and looks like a psychopath.

So—with Dad's permission—we put the film in and watched it.

This would turn out to be the single most important thing ever to happen in our lives.

It was incredible. It was confusing, and terrifying, and incredible. We had to pause it every time there were subtitles, and a bunch of times we had to run out to get Dad to explain something or another, and eventually Dad came in to watch it with us, and it was *still* incredible.

Dad being there was actually a big help. He read the subtitles out loud and answered questions we had about the

plot, and we had a lot of questions, because everyone in the film is insane.

Again: It was incredible. It was like nothing either of us had ever experienced. It was funny, and it was grim. There was a lot of death, but it wasn't like video-game death. It was slower, and bloodier, and less frequent. In GoldenEye, you see someone get shot, and you watch them fall backward and crumple on the ground; here, you would just suddenly find a body. The randomness of it blew us away. Every time someone died we yelled, "Oh *snap*." And the suspense was unbelievable. Klaus Kinski doesn't lose it and kill anyone for the entire first half hour. Then, even when he does, he acts like it was no big deal, and you have no idea when he's going to do it again. He has this unpredictable, psychopath brain that you can't read. It got us so fired up.

We loved all of it. We loved how slow it was. We loved that it took forever. Actually, we never wanted it to end. We loved the jungle, the rafts, the ridiculous armor and helmets. We loved that it sort of felt like a home movie, like it all actually *happened* and someone on the raft just happened to have a camera. I think most of all we loved that it didn't have a happy ending for *anyone.* The whole time, we were sort of expecting that someone would survive, because that's how stories work: Even if everything is a total disaster, someone lives to tell the tale. But not with *Aguirre, the Wrath of God.* Hell no. *Everyone* dies. That's awesome.

Also, the movie had the first breasts I had ever seen, although they were not what I had been led to believe that breasts looked like. They were like cow udders, and one of them was bigger than the other. (In retrospect, this may have been responsible for my complete lack of sexual development, which we've already talked about. I guess at least I wasn't going around saying things like, "The best thing about your two boobs is that they are the same size.")

Afterward we asked Dad a bunch of questions about it, and somehow we got to talking about the *making* of the film, and apparently it was a total disaster. People got sick, the entire cast and crew got stranded in the jungle for months, and some of the crew might have died. Dad wasn't sure. Best of all, the actor Klaus Kinski himself was just as crazy in real life as he was as Aguirre. He actually shot one of the other guys working on the film. It was because he was being too noisy, and Kinski wanted to concentrate. So he shot his crewmate *in the hand with a gun.* If that doesn't make you drop this book and go watch the movie right now, I don't even know what's wrong with you. Maybe *you* have a brain fungus.

Obviously, we had to watch it again. Dad wasn't up for another round, but we thought it was even better the second time. We imitated the German voices, especially Kinski's, who talked like he was being strangled. We imitated Kinski's drunken staggering walk. We lay around the house for hours pretending to be dead, until Gretchen found one of us and had her own mini freak-out and started crying uncontrollably.

In short, we decided that it was the greatest film ever made. And the next weekend, we invited some classmates over to share it with them.

They hated it.

We didn't even make it past the first twenty minutes. They said it was too slow. They couldn't read the subtitles, and we

weren't good enough at reading them out loud. The speech at the beginning by Pizarro, they said, was long and boring. The plot of the movie seemed stupid to them: Aguirre and everyone were searching for a city that *it said right at the beginning did not exist.* They didn't understand that that was *the whole point.* They didn't get that it was awesome *because* it was so insanely meaningless. Instead, they kept calling it gay.

It was a disaster, but it was also useful. It made us conscious of what we had really known all along: We were different from the other kids. We had different interests, a different kind of focus. It's hard to explain. Earl and I actually didn't have much in common with each other, either, but we were the only ten-year-olds in Pittsburgh who liked *Aguirre, the Wrath of God,* and that counted for something. It actually counted for a lot.

"The young nihilists," Dad called us.

"What are nihilists?"

"Nihilists believe that nothing has any meaning. They believe in nothing."

"Yeah," said Earl. "I'm a nihilist."

"Me, too," I said.

"Good for you," Dad said, grinning. Then he stopped grinning and said, "Don't tell your mom."

And that's part of the backstory for me and Earl. It'll probably be relevant later, although who really knows. I can't believe you're still reading this. You should smack yourself in the face a couple of times right now, just to complete the outstandingly stupid experience that is this book.

Chapter 12

I PUT THE "IDIOT" IN "VIDEOTAPE"

One thing I've learned about people is that the easiest way to get them to like you is to shut up and let them do the talking. Everyone likes to talk about themselves. It's not just kids whose lives are good. Take Jared "Crackhead" Krakievich, one of Benson's scrawniest and least popular students. As far as I know, Jared has never done crack, but he walks around with his arms dangling awkwardly behind the rest of his body kind of like a chicken, his mouth is always hanging at least three-quarters open, and there is usually food in his braces. He smells like pickles and his parents are yinzers. You'd think he wouldn't want to talk about his life, but you'd be wrong, as I discovered one day on the bus. For example, I learned that his dog can tell when Ben Roethlisberger is about to get sacked, and that he (Jared, not the dog or Ben Roethlisberger) was thinking about learning to play guitar.

If you're not from Pittsburgh, I should probably explain that "yinzers" are people with heavy Pittsburgh accents. For example, instead of "you" or "y'all," they say "yinz." Another feature of

yinzers is that they wear Steelers apparel at all times, including in the workplace and at weddings.

Basically, my point is not that you listen to people to learn anything interesting. You're doing it to be nice and make them like you, because everyone likes to talk.

But this theory did not apply to Rachel, somehow. I would go to her house determined to get her to do the talking, and then I'd show up and pretty soon I would be talking more than someone who was on crystal meth.

INT. RACHEL'S BEDROOM — DAY

The second or third time that GREG has gone over to RACHEL'S. Both are sitting cross-legged on the floor.

                    GREG
        So. What TV do you like watching?

                    RACHEL
        Whatever's on, I guess.

                    GREG
              unnerved by the calm blankness
              of this response
        So, like. Nature shows? Reality
        shows? Just, everything's fair game?

                    RACHEL
          Yeah, pretty much.

                    GREG
          Not the Food Network though.

Rachel shrugs.

                    GREG
          Here's my thing with the Food Network:
          OK, half the time the food looks
          gross, or weird. It's covered in weird
          sauce that looks like semen, or it's
          squid in a goat hoof or something.
          But then, the other half of the time,
          if it's something *good,* and people eat
          it, and they're like, *Mmmmm,* this is
          delicious — that's even worse! Because
          you don't get to eat it. You're just
          watching these people eat something
          delicious, and you don't even get to
          know what it tastes like, and you
          want to kill yourself. But most of
          the time the food doesn't look
          that good.

RACHEL

diplomatically

Some people think it looks good.

GREG

OK, but then here's the other thing:
It's always a food *competition*. Food
isn't a sport. It's ridiculous for
cooks to be competing against each
other. Like in *Iron Chef*, it always
takes place in Kitchen Stadium.
Kitchen *Stadium*? That's ridiculous.
And at the end it's always like,
You have competed honorably. How is
it possible to be *dishonorable*? You
were making a *stew*.

RACHEL

giggling

Hmmmm.

GREG

I mean, if the Food Network can
turn *food* into a sport, why draw
the line there? You know? "*Iron
Plumber*, tonight at Toilet Arena."

Or, or, no wait. Wait, forget that
one. "Live, from Toilet Center: *Super
Poopers*."

Four hours later. Greg and Rachel are in
EXACTLY THE SAME POSITION.

>   GREG
> . . . I guess my point is just that,
> it's weird that we have animals
> living in our homes. It's just weird.

>   RACHEL
> I should probably go eat dinner.

>   GREG
>   *alarmed*
> Wait, what time is it?

>   RACHEL
> It's around eight.

>   GREG
> Holy fuck.

In her quiet way, Rachel was actually being sort of brilliant.

89

1. Rachel was using my own tactics against me. Props to her. This is some high-concept judo behavior. She orchestrated our conversations so that I did the talking and she did the listening. Sure enough, this made me like spending time with her. I told you this tactic is awesome. Also, she kicked ass at listening. I mean, in her position, I would have gotten really bored or annoyed. *Super Poopers*, Greg? Christ.

2. Rachel was not suggesting that we had to make out or get married. Even though I had told her that I had been deeply in love with her, she was not trying to make up for lost time. This probably would have caused me to freak out and maybe fake having a serious mental disorder, which is a tactic that I have considered from time to time to get out of situations. If I ever got jumped in the locker room by jocks, for example. On TV, jocks like to harass kids with mental disorders, but in real life, I've observed that everyone pretty much just wants to stay away from them. Anyway, I was worried this would become necessary with Rachel, but thank God it did not.

3. By getting me to talk so much, Rachel was eventually going to get me to divulge sensitive information that would ultimately lead to my downfall. Am I giving too much away? Maybe I'm giving too much away.

```
INT. RACHEL'S BEDROOM — DAY

GREG'S third or fourth time at RACHEL'S.
```

Greg has noticed that one of the pictures
of HUGH JACKMAN is sort of wall-eyed, and
one of the EYES is following him around
the room. Rachel has just stopped talking.

>   GREG
>   *distracted*
> What?

>   RACHEL
> I wasn't really saying anything
> important.

>   GREG
> Sorry, Hugh Jackman's creepy right
> eye is following me around your room.

>   RACHEL
> He's not creepy!

>   GREG
> What were we talking about?

>   RACHEL
> Hebrew school.

>   GREG
> Right. What a waste.

RACHEL

You think?

GREG

I learned nothing. Seriously, I can't
tell you anything about Jews. I *am* a Jew,
and I still deserve an F in Jewishness.

RACHEL

I think it's "Judaism."

GREG

See, that's what I'm talking about.
I don't even know what to call it.
And I definitely don't know what Jews
believe. Like, do Jews believe in
heaven? Are we supposed to believe
in that?

RACHEL

I don't know.

GREG

Yeah. Is there Jewish heaven? What
happens when Jews die? You know?

HUGH JACKMAN is glaring at Greg.

                    GREG
Oh shit.

                    RACHEL
What?

                    GREG
          hastily
Uh, nothing. Sorry, I'm an idiot.

                    RACHEL
For what?

                    GREG
Uh.
          about as stupidly as it is
          possible to say words
The death thing.

                    RACHEL
Greg. I'm not *dying*.

                    GREG
          lying
Yeah, I know.

> RACHEL
> *narrowing eyes*
> I'm *sick*, but everyone gets sick.
> Just because you're sick doesn't
> mean you're going to die.

> GREG
> *falsely*
> Yeah yeah yeah yeah, no, yeah.

> RACHEL
> You think I'm about to die.

> GREG
> *just lying his ass off*
> No! No-o-o-o-o.

> RACHEL
> *warily*
> Huh.

INT. RACHEL'S BEDROOM — DAY

GREG'S fourth or fifth time at RACHEL'S.
Greg is on the bed with his back to HUGH
JACKMAN, although that means he has to
face DANIEL CRAIG in a Speedo with a big
goofy smile on his face.

DANIEL CRAIG

You can see the outline of my
genitals! Isn't this *great?*

RACHEL
giggling
That's not what Daniel Craig even
sounds like.

GREG

I have to warm up. I'm not in Accent
Mode.

RACHEL

That sounded like a cowboy accent.

GREG

Yeah, I was using the wrong part
of my mouth. Accents are all about
using certain parts of your mouth.
That's why foreign people's faces
are sometimes kind of jacked up. Like
how Daniel Craig has those weird
pouty lips like a woman.

RACHEL

He *does not.*

GREG

Look at him! Look how he's sticking
his lips out. Actually he sort of
looks like a frog.

    launching into autopilot
    because Rachel is remaining
    silent/expectant

I just know a lot about accents, even
if I can't do them. I've studied them.
I mean I've seen a lot of films. A
cool thing about accents actually is
the way they change from like eighty
years ago to forty years ago to now,
if you watch movies that are older.
People's mouths were just shaped
differently back then, I think.

Sometimes I want to walk around doing
an American accent from the 1950s,
because that in some ways is the
weirdest accent there is. You really
freak people out that way. When
people hear it, they don't think,
1950s; they think, that guy sounds
all weird and rigid and conservative,
like an asshole robot, and they don't
know why.

I mean, I had to watch a bunch
of films from back then before I
realized that people just talked
differently.

                    RACHEL
So you're really like a movie expert.

                    GREG
I'm not an expert. I've just seen a
whole lot of them.

                    RACHEL
What's your favorite movie?

INT. THE GAINES TV ROOM — TWO HOURS LATER

On the screen: KLAUS KINSKI. On the couch:
RACHEL and GREG. On Greg's lap: a bowl
containing leftover BEEF TIPS that he
found in the fridge.

                    GREG
See how the camera's moving around,
sort of jittery, like it's handheld?
OK. Do you sort of get how it makes
the film feel less like fiction and

more like it really happened? You
know what I mean?

RACHEL
Yeah, I think so.

GREG
It's awesome, right? It feels that
way because it feels a little like
a documentary. Because that's
the camerawork that you have in a
documentary, lots of handheld, no
huge smooth crane shots like in big
action movies.

RACHEL
It feels a little like reality TV.

GREG
Yeah! That too. Well, except the
lighting in reality TV is always
really unnatural, and here, they
really can't bring a lot of
artificial lights into the jungle.
Actually, they might not have
anything besides reflectors.

                    RACHEL
What are reflectors?

                    GREG
               gnawing beef
Mmmrflectors urmmff . . . hang on,
this scene is awesome.

                    RACHEL
You should try making some movies.

                    MOM
               from doorway
He does! He just doesn't let
anyone see them.

                    GREG
MOM WHAT THE HELL ARE YOU DOING

                    MOM
Oh honey. Did you not offer Rachel
anything to eat?

                    GREG
JESUS MOM

                    RACHEL
I'm not hungry!

GREG

infuriated

Mom. Jesus Christ. You can't just
spy on us from the doorway. And you
def

MOM

I was just *walking past* and I heard
Rach

GREG

initely can't just tell people about,
um,

RACHEL

It's

MOM

Greg, you're being a little silly
abou

GREG

s stuff that you *know* is really priv

AGUIRRE

*When I wish for the birds to fall
from the trees, then shall the birds
fall from the trees.*

                    MOM
ou work so hard on these movies with
Earl and then y

                    RACHEL
It's OK, I don't need to see them.

                    GREG
See? Did you hear that?

                    MOM
just keep them to yourselves like
you don't wan

                    GREG
Did you — *Mom*. Did you hear what
Rachel said.

                    MOM
She's just being nice. Greg, you
have some juice on your chin.

                    GREG
Will you *please just get out of
here.*

MOM exits, smiling wryly, like she just
did something clever and wasn't in fact a

HORRIBLE MOTHER. Meanwhile, Greg is back to eating beef tips, because when he is stressed out he eats compulsively.

> RACHEL
> Here, let's rewind it. I think we missed an important part.

> GREG
> Yeah, it's like the best part.

> RACHEL
> *after a lengthy silence*
> If your movies are secret, I won't tell anyone. You can trust me.

> GREG
> *frustrated*
> It's not that they're *secret*, it's just that they're not good enough for people to see. Once we do a really good one, we'll let people see it.

> RACHEL
> That makes sense.

> GREG
> What?

RACHEL

I understand.

GREG

Oh.

They look into each other's eyes.

If this were a touching romantic story,
in this moment some STRANGE NEW FEELING
would wash over Greg — a sense of being
understood, in a basic way that he almost
never is understood. Then, Greg and Rachel
would make out like lovesick badgers.

However, this is not a touching romantic
story. There is no NEW FEELING that washes
over Greg. There is no BADGER MAKE-OUT
SESSION.

Instead, Greg sort of shifts uncomfortably
and breaks eye contact.

RACHEL

Can I get you a napkin or something?

GREG

No no I'll get it.

Chapter 13

EVEN MORE
EARL BACKSTORY

The first film Earl and I remade was *Aguirre, the Wrath of God*. Obviously. It couldn't have been any other one. We were eleven, and we had seen it approximately thirty times, to the point where we had memorized all of the subtitles and even some of the dialogue in German. We sometimes repeated it in class, when the teacher asked us questions. Earl especially did this a lot, if he didn't know the answer.

```
INT. MRS. WOZNIEWSKI'S FIFTH GRADE
CLASS — DAY

                    MRS. WOZNIEWSKI
        Earl, can you name some layers of
        the earth?

EARL's eyes bug out. He breathes
hard through his nose.
```

MRS. WOZNIEWSKI

Let's start with the one on the
inside. What's another word for —

EARL

Ich bin der große Verräter.
[subtitle: I am the great traitor.]

MRS. WOZNIEWSKI

Hmmm.

EARL

Die Erde über die ich gehe sieht
mich und bebt.
[subtitle: The earth I walk upon
sees me and trembles.]*

MRS. WOZNIEWSKI

Earl, do you want to tell us what
that means?

EARL

glowering at classmates
grrrrhh

MRS. WOZNIEWSKI

Earl.

           EARL

     standing up, pointing to MRS.

     WOZNIEWSKI, addressing class

  Der Mann ist einen Kopf größer als ich.

  DAS KANN SICH ÄNDERN.

  [subtitle: That man is a head taller

  than me. THAT CAN CHANGE.*]*

          MRS. WOZNIEWSKI

  Earl, please go sit in the hall.

And then one day Dad bought a video camera and some editing software for his computer. It was to videotape his lectures or something. We didn't know the specifics; we knew only that the specifics were boring. We knew also that this technology had come into our lives for a reason: We had to re-create every single shot in *Aguirre, the Wrath of God.*

We figured it would take about an afternoon. Instead, it took three months, and when I say "it," I mean, "re-creating the first ten minutes and then giving up." Like Werner Herzog in the South American jungle, we faced almost unimaginable setbacks and difficulties. We kept taping over our own footage, or not hitting record, or running out of camera battery. We didn't really know how the lighting or sound was supposed to work. Some of the cast members—mostly Gretchen—proved incapable of delivering their lines properly, or staying in character, or not picking their nose. Also, we usually had a cast of just three people, or two if someone needed to hold the camera. The location we used was Frick Park, and joggers and dog walkers kept entering the shot, and then they would make things even worse by trying to start a conversation.

Q: Are you guys shooting a movie?
A: No. We're opening a mid-priced Italian restaurant.
Q: Huh?
A: *Yes of course we're shooting a movie.*
Q: What's the movie about?
A: It's a documentary about human stupidity.
Q: Can I be in your movie?
A: *We'd* be stupid *not* to put you in it.

Moreover, props and costumes were impossible to replicate. Earl wore a pot on his head, and it looked ridiculous. Nothing we had looked like cannons, or swords. Mom said we weren't allowed to bring furniture from the house to the park, and then when we did, we had Suspended Camera Privileges for a week.

Also, our process was dumb as all hell. We'd get to the forest and then completely forget what shot we were working on, or if we remembered it, we couldn't remember the lines, and how the camera moved, and where the characters started and where they ended; we'd struggle for a while to shoot something that we thought was correct, without success. Finally, we'd go back to the house to try to write down what we were supposed to do, but then we'd end up having lunch or watching a movie or something; at the end of the day we'd try to get everything on the computer, but there was always some footage missing, and the

scenes that survived looked like crap—bad lighting, inaudible dialogue, shaky camerawork.

So we did this for months, eventually realized how slow we were working, and gave up after creating ten minutes of footage.

Then Mom and Dad insisted on watching what we had done.

It was a nightmare. For ten minutes, Earl and I watched with horror as, on the screen, we wandered around waving cardboard tubes and Super Soakers, mumbling in fake German, ignoring cheerful joggers and families and senior citizens with beagles. We had already known it was bad, but somehow, with Mom and Dad there watching, it seemed ten times worse. We became aware of new ways in which it was crappy: how there wasn't really a plot, for example, and how we forgot to put in music, and how you couldn't see anything half the time and Gretchen pretty much just stared at the camera like a house pet and Earl obviously hadn't memorized his lines and I always always *always* had this stupid expression on my face like I had just had a lobotomy. And the worst part was, *Mom and Dad were pretending to like it.* They kept telling us how impressive it was, how well we had acted in it, how they couldn't believe we had made something so good. They were literally oohing and ahhing at the stupid garbage on the screen.

Basically, they were dealing with us as though we were toddlers. I wanted to murder myself. Earl did, too. Instead, we just sat there and didn't say anything.

Afterward we retreated to my room, utterly bummed out.

INT. MY ROOM — DAY

                    EARL
     Damn. That sucked.

                    GREG
     We suck.

                    EARL
     I fuckin suck worse than you do.

                    GREG
          attempting to match the
          casualness with which eleven-
          year-old Earl can say words
          like "fuck"
     Uh, shit.

                    EARL
     Fuck.

                    DAD
          offscreen, through the door
     Guys, dinner's in ten minutes.
          after we do not reply
     Guys? That was really pretty amazing.
     Mom and I are very impressed. You both
     should be really proud of yourselves.

a shorter pause
You guys all right? Can I come in there?

EARL
immediately
Hell no.

GREG
We're OK, Dad.

EARL
If he come in here and talk about that
stupid movie, I'ma kick myself in the head.

DAD
OK then!

Footsteps indicate that DAD has left.

GREG
That sucked so bad.

EARL
I'ma get that tape and burn it.

GREG
*still having trouble swearing
convincingly*

Yeah, uh, fuck. Shit.

GREG and EARL are silent. CLOSE-UP of
Earl. Earl is realizing something.

> EARL
> Werner Herzog can lick my ass-cheek.

> GREG

What?

> EARL
> Man, fuck *Aguirre, the Wrath of God*.
> Werner Herzog can stick his face all
> up in my butthole.

> GREG
> *uncertainly*

OK.

> EARL
> We gotta make our *own* movie.
> *gaining momentum*
> We can't try to make someone else's
> movie. We're gonna make our *own* movie.
> *now excited*
> We're gonna make a movie called *The
> Wrath of God II*.

GREG

Earl, the Wrath of God II.

EARL

HELL YEAH.

In our creative partnership, Earl has always had the best ideas, and *Earl, the Wrath of God II* was one of his best. It never would have occurred to me, even though it wasn't that complicated or crazy of an idea: Basically, it was to remake *Aguirre* again, but this time, to change all the parts that we couldn't do, or even just the parts that we didn't feel like doing. If there was a scene we didn't like, in our version, it was gone. A character we couldn't re-create: *sayonara*. A jungle that we couldn't reproduce: converted into a living room, or the inside of a car. The best ideas are always the simplest.

So *Earl, the Wrath of God II* ended up being about a crazy guy named Earl and his search for the city of Earl Dorado *in a normal family house in Pittsburgh.* We shot it on location in the Gaines residence in Point Breeze, and we ad-libbed a lot of the dialogue, and Cat Stevens made some awesome cameos, and we set the whole thing to a funk CD Dad had lying around, and it took another month or two. At the end of it, we burned it to a DVD and had a secret viewing of the movie in the TV room.

It sucked. But it didn't suck nearly as bad as our first film.

Our careers were born.

Chapter 14

CAFETERIORATION

So by October things were weird. I had a person, at school, that I was being especially nice to and spending time with and stuff. Could we use the word "friend"? I guess. Rachel was my friend. You should know that writing that sentence didn't feel good. It just didn't. Having friends is how your life gets fucked up.

Anyway, I couldn't keep ignoring her in school when we were spending all this time together outside of school, so all of a sudden, in school, I was seen having a friend. I was seen by everyone talking to Rachel before and after class, and often this resulted in her laughing kind of loud, and that got people's attention. And when it was time to work in groups, we were almost always in the same group. And people notice stuff like that.

So probably some people thought we were boyfriend and girlfriend, and perhaps even having sex. And how can you fight that impression without seeming like a dick? You can't go around making remarks like, "There's certainly nothing going on between me and Rachel! Especially nothing sexual. I don't even

know what her genital area looks like, or if it's in a different place than normal or something."

At the very least, people thought we were casually dating. And here's the thing: Most people, especially girls, seemed to get fired up about that. I have a theory about that, and the theory is depressing.

Theory: People always get fired up when an unattractive girl and an unattractive dude are dating each other.

No one came out and said anything to this effect, but I feel like it's probably true. When girls see two Unattractives dating, they think, "Hey! Love is possible even for unattractive people. They have to love different things about each other than their physical appearances. That's so sweet." Meanwhile, dudes see it and think, "That is *one less guy* I have to compete with for the most succulent boobs in the Boob Competition that is high school."

And, inevitably, spending time with Rachel meant being at least partially absorbed by her group, Upper-Middle-Class Senior Jewish Girl Sub-Clique 2a: Rachel Kushner, Naomi Shapiro, and Anna Tuchman. Naomi Shapiro had this loud, blustering, sarcastic persona that she used at all times, and Anna Tuchman was OK but invariably clutching a paperback with a title like *The Meridian Sword* or *Cleavage of Destiny* or something. A few times before school, I was roped into spending time with these girls. Their conversations were tough to be part of for a sustained period of time.

INT. BENSON HALLWAY — MORNING

                    ANNA
        Ugggh. I don't want to go to English
        today.

                    NAOMI
        MR. CUBALY IS SUCH A PERV.

Giggling from RACHEL and ANNA.

                    NAOMI
                pretending not to understand
                the giggling
        WHAT?! HE'S ALWAYS TRYING TO LOOK
        DOWN MY SHIRT.

More giggling. GREG is also politely
trying to giggle and failing.

                    NAOMI
        IT'S LIKE: TAKE A PICTURE, MR.
        CUBALY, IT'LL LAST LONGER.

                    ANNA
                pretending to be horrified
        Naomi-i-i-i-i-i!!

All of a sudden everyone is looking at
Greg to see what *he* thinks of all this.

> GREG
> *deciding that the safest option*
> *is simply to summarize what has*
> *been said thus far*
> Uh . . . Takin' a picture of some
> boobs. Cubaly style.

> NAOMI
> UGGGGGH. BOYS ARE SUCH PERVERTS.
> GREG, CAN YOU THINK ABOUT JUST ONE
> THING OTHER THAN SEX.

> ENTIRE HALLWAY'S
> WORTH OF STUDENTS
> Greg, we are all making a note of
> your playful bantering friendship
> with this loud obnoxious person.

So yeah, my hard-earned social invisibility definitely was
taking something of a hit. I even made the mistake one afternoon
of agreeing to have lunch with Rachel and her friends in the
cafeteria, a place I hadn't set foot in for years.

The cafeteria is chaos. First of all, it's in a perpetual state of
low-level food fight. It's rarely violent enough for the security
guards to get involved, but at any given time, someone is

attempting to whip a piece of food or condiment at someone else from close range, and half of the time they miss and hit someone else in a different part of the cafeteria. So it's like one of the more chill battles of World War II.

Second of all, the food every single day is pizza and Tater Tots. Sometimes to mix things up they put little gray poop-like nuggets of sausage on the pizza, but that's as much variation as there is. Also, a lot of food ends up on the cafeteria floor, and both pizza and Tater Tots get very slippery when stepped on. There's also a lot of dried Pepsi down there, which is sticky and therefore easy to walk on but somehow even more disgusting.

Finally, the cafeteria is extremely crowded, meaning if you accidentally slip on a slick of pizza cheese and mashed-up Tater Tots, you will probably be trampled to death.

Basically, it's like a low-security state prison.

And so I had to sit there with my backpack perched awkwardly on my lap, because you do not want your backpack down there under the table accumulating greasy food stains and families of insects, and I was eating my weird but probably healthful lunch that Dad had packed because if I ate pizza and Tater Tots every day I would be even more overweight and my face would have a pimple somewhere the size of a human eyeball. And Naomi was loudly talking about how Ross Said Something Ignorant and I Was Like Don't Even Go There, and I was attempting to listen politely and probably had some kind of dumb smile or grimace on my face. And that's the state I was in when Madison Hartner came over to sit with us.

So in case you don't remember, Madison Hartner is the insanely hot girl who probably dates one of the Pittsburgh Steelers or at least a college student or something. She's also the girl that I relentlessly antagonized in the fifth grade, with the Madison Fartner nickname, the Booger ChapStick accusation, etc. That's all water under the bridge now, of course, and in October of senior year, we were on vaguely friendly terms with each other. We would say hi to each other in the hall sometimes, and maybe I would even make some kind of bland inoffensive joke, and she would smile or something, and I would daydream for a couple of seconds about nuzzling my face in her boobs like an affectionate panda cub, and then we would both get on with our lives.

Did I want to get with Madison? Yes. Of course I did. I would have given up a year of my life just to make out with her. Well, maybe a month. And obviously she would have to be doing it voluntarily. I'm not suggesting that some weird wish-granting genie would force her to make out with me in exchange for a month of my life. This entire paragraph is a moron.

Look: If you asked me, Greg, who do you have a crush on, the answer would be Madison. But most of the time I was able to not think about girls, because in high school guys like me are completely unable to get with the girls they actually want to get with, so there's no sense in dwelling on that like a pathetic idiot.

I asked Dad point-blank about girls in high school once and he said that, yeah, high school is impossible, but college is different and that once I get there I "should have no trouble making whoopie," which was embarrassing but reassuring at the same time. Then I asked Mom and she said I'm actually very handsome, and that statement immediately became Piece of Evidence #16087 in the case of *Mom v. The Truth.*

Anyway. Madison, a hot and almost universally popular girl, came strolling up to us and plunked her tray down next to Rachel's. Why did she choose to do this? Here, let me give you another long-winded explanation of something. I am like the Joseph Stalin of narrators.

There are two kinds of hot girls: Evil Hot Girls, and Hot Girls Who Are Also Sympathetic Good-Hearted People and Will Not Intentionally Destroy Your Life (HGWAASGHPAWNIDYL). Olivia Ryan—the first girl in our class to get a nose job—is definitely an Evil Hot Girl, which is why everyone is terrified of her. Periodically she will just randomly destroy someone's life. Occasionally it's because that person wrote something on Facebook like liv ryan is a btichhhh !!!! but most of the time, there's no reason for it. It's like a volcano suddenly erupted in someone's house and melted their flesh. At Benson, I would estimate that about 75 percent of hot girls are evil.

But Madison Hartner is not evil. Actually, she's like the president of the HGWAASGHPAWNIDYL. The best evidence of this is Rachel. Madison and Rachel were, at best, distant acquaintances before Rachel got cancer, but when the cancer happened, this triggered Madison's Friend Hormones.

Let me also tell you that the problem with HGWAAS-GHPAWNIDYL is, just because they're not intentionally out to destroy your life, doesn't mean they don't sometimes still destroy

your life. They can't help it. They're like elephants, blithely roaming the jungle, occasionally stomping a chipmunk and not even noticing: hot, sexy elephants.

Actually, Madison is a lot like Mom. She's obsessed with doing Good Deeds, and she's awesome at persuading people to do stuff. This is just an incredibly dangerous combination, as you will see later in this book, if I can even finish it without freaking out and throwing my laptop out of a moving car and into a pond.

All right. So Madison's leukemia-activated Friend Hormones had begun pumping through her system, and now she was showing her friendship by sitting with us during lunch.

"Is anyone sitting here?" she asked. She has this dark honeyed kind of wise-sounding voice, which doesn't quite fit how she looks. That is also hot. I feel like an assclown writing about how hot she is, so I'll stop.

"I DON'T THINK SO," said Naomi.

"Sit with us," said Rachel.

So she sat there. Naomi was being quiet. The balance of power had shifted in ways that none of us yet understood. There was tension in the air. It was a moment of great opportunity, and greater danger. The world was about to change forever. I had beef in my mouth.

"Greg, that looks like an interesting lunch," said Madison.

Lunch was leftover beef slices, bean sprouts, and lettuce in a plastic container. There was also teriyaki sauce and scallions and stuff. It basically looked like an alien came to earth and took a class in salad-making but didn't do all that great on the final exam. Anyway, this was my opportunity, and I seized it.

"I already *had* lunch," I said. "This is the barf of a space alien."

Rachel and Anna snorted, and *Madison actually giggled a little bit.* I did not have time to truly register the boner-generating ramifications of that, because Naomi was clearly about to make a loud irritating attempt to reclaim the center of attention, and I had to prevent this at all costs.

"Yeah, for extra credit in Mr. McCarthy's class, I'm doing a documentary on the barfing habits of space aliens. I follow them around with a camera, and I collect their barf in containers like this. You thought I was going to *eat* this? No way. Madison, you must think I'm perverted. I'm a *barf historian*, and you need to have some respect for that. That's why I have this beautiful specimen of barf in this container here. *I'm* going to do some *research* with it."

Naomi was periodically trying to cut in by bellowing "GROSS" and "YOU DID NOT JUST GO THERE," but to no avail. I was getting some momentum and had some decent laughs going, especially from Rachel, who at that point was the Duchess of Snortsylvania.

"I am *not* going to eat this precious barf. Let me explain something to you guys. When an alien barfs, it's a sign of trust. I have spent a *ton* of time with aliens, gaining their trust so that they can bestow their wondrous barf on me, and I am *not* about to sabotage that trust by eating the barf. Even though it looks nutritious and like it would taste awesome. Check it out. Look

at these weird sperm-looking thingies. Do they make me want to just go to town on this barf? And eat it in my mouth? *Obviously.* But this is about *trust.* Next question. Rachel."

Rachel was helplessly snorting and honking away, so I knew if I gave her the opportunity to speak, it would let me reload a little bit without letting Naomi talk. I was also trying not to focus on the fact that I was making probably Benson's hottest girl laugh. This was easily the only time anything like this had ever happened.

"Where do you even *find* space aliens," Rachel eventually managed to ask.

"Awesome question," I said. "Space aliens generally disguise themselves as people, but if you know what to look for, you can identify them pretty easily." I was sort of looking around the cafeteria for inspiration. For some reason I was focusing on Scott Mayhew, one of the Magic-card-playing gothy dorks from eighteen thousand words ago. He was wearing a trench coat and he was clumsily loping around with a school lunch tray.

"Aliens have an unusual fashion sense revolving around trench coats," I continued, "and they haven't really figured out how to use human legs to walk normally. Like, don't look now, but Scott Mayhew over there? Yeah. He is a textbook alien."

My heart was racing. On the one hand, I had just committed a cardinal sin of my whole way of being: *Never make fun of anybody.* Talking shit on people is probably the easiest way to make friends and enemies in high school, or really anywhere, and as I have noted like a billion times, that is the opposite of my goal in life.

But on the other hand, I had three girls cracking up, and one of them was Madison, and another was Rachel, and I had to keep it going.

"You've probably seen Scott running around all weird and stuff, and you've thought to yourself, what is his deal. Well, he's from outer space. His home is on some fucked-up meteor or something. And it's taken a really long time for us to get to the *level of trust* where he'll let me carry around his barf. You don't even want to know how much alien poetry I've had to sit around and listen to. It's mostly about centaurs. And finally this morning after he read me some of his poetry, I was like, 'I'd like to thank you for that, that was really beautiful,' and then he was like, '*I'd* like to honor you with my *barf.*' And that's when he barfed in this thing here. It's been a wild ride."

And then I shut up, because Scott had sort of stopped what he was doing and was staring at us from across the cafeteria. He can't have liked what he was seeing. Anna, Rachel, and Madison were all looking at him and laughing. And I was saying things with a big dumb grin on my face. He knew we were making fun of him. It was obvious. He gazed at me coldly and angrily.

"GREG, YOU'RE WEIRD AND GROSS," announced Naomi, stepping eagerly into the void.

"Greg, you're being mean," said Madison with a sweet smile on her face.

How the hell was I going to get out of this. "No, no, no!" I yelled. "Naomi, alien barf is not gross. That's the whole *point.* It's rare and beautiful. And Madison, what I'm saying is not *mean.* It's like the opposite. I'm *celebrating* this magical bond that Scott

and I have. With his barf. That I'm holding right now in this container."

But I was freaked out. I had temporarily lost control of myself and talked shit on Scott Mayhew and made him probably hate me. And also now I had created a reputation for myself as a guy who talks shit on people. I was so freaked out that I didn't even really say anything else until the bell rang for next period, and of course in the weeks to follow, I did not return to the cafeteria. I couldn't even think about eating lunch down there without my armpits getting all hot and prickly.

Later, Rachel confided to me that Scott Mayhew had a big crush on Anna.

"Ohhh. That makes sense."

"Really?"

"Yeah. She's always reading books about centaurs and stuff."

"I think he's too weird for her."

"He's not that weird."

I was still feeling guilty and sensitive about the whole Scott thing.

"Greg, he's pretty weird. And his hair is gross."

"Well, he's not as weird as *me*."

"I guess you're the one making the space alien barf documentary."

"Yeah."

"Are your other films documentaries?"

I think Rachel was trying to give me an opportunity to go on some open-ended riff about something here, but honestly I was too freaked out to really say anything. There was the Scott thing, and now there was Rachel bringing up my films, and I just didn't know what to do.

So I kind of just said, "Uhhhhh. Not really. Uh."

But fortunately Rachel understood what this meant.

"Sorry, I know they're secret. I shouldn't ask you about them."

"No, I'm being stupid."

"No you're not. It's important to you that they're secret. I don't want you to describe them to me."

I have to say this: In that moment, Rachel was awesome. Meanwhile, I guess I probably have to describe the films to *you.* You're being less awesome than Rachel, you stupid reader.

I mean, I'm the one who's deciding you have to read about them, so really it's me who is being a human poop factory right now.

This should come as a surprise to no one.

Chapter 15

GAINES/JACKSON: THE COLLECTED WORKS

This is obviously just a partial list.

Earl, the Wrath of God II (dir. G. Gaines and E. Jackson, 2005). Yes, I know. The *II* makes no sense. It should have been either *Aguirre, the Wrath of God II,* or *Earl, the Wrath of God I.* Whatever. At the time, *Earl, the Wrath of God II* just seemed to work. Also, we were eleven. Give us a break.

Anyway, Earl's bravura performance as a psychotic fake-German-speaking Spanish conquistador was overshadowed by a near-total lack of plot, character development, intelligible dialogue, etc. In hindsight, we probably should have used less footage of Cat Stevens flipping out and attacking one of us. We also should have added subtitles, because there is no way to tell what Earl is trying to say. *"Ich haufen mit staufen ZAUFENSTEINNN,"* for example. It sounds great, but literally translated, it means "I pile/cluster/accumulation with [nonsense word] ALCOHOL-DRINKING-STONNNNE." ★

Ran II (dir. G. Gaines and E. Jackson, 2006). We really stepped it up for *Ran II*, with costumes, a soundtrack, weaponry, and a plot that we actually sat and tried to write down beforehand. Here goes: An emperor and his sons are having dinner. One of the sons makes fun of the emperor. The emperor becomes enraged and kills his own court jester. The wife of one of the other sons runs in and announces that she has just gotten remarried to another emperor. She is noogied to death. The second emperor, meanwhile, lives in a bathroom and eats soap, and has a lengthy freak-out scene when a messenger tells him that his wife is dead. The messenger turns out to be the rebellious son; the rebellious son, however, then makes the mistake of walking under a tree, where a mysterious assassin is waiting with some toothpaste. The assassin and the first emperor chase each other through the forest for a while. This causes the second emperor to have an even longer freak-out scene. Eventually, he runs into the living room and commits Elbow-Forehead Suicide, while the for-some-reason-alive-again court jester sings a very loud nonsense song.

And that's when things get complicated. ★★

Apocalypse Later (dir. G. Gaines and E. Jackson, 2007). Again, not our best title. Once we found out what the apocalypse was, we thought that it was ridiculous that *Apocalypse Now* was not, in fact, about the End of the World. This movie can best be summed up like this:

1. Earl, wearing a bandanna and holding a Super Soaker, demands to know when the apocalypse is happening.

2. Offscreen, I tell Earl that the apocalypse is not for a while.

3. Earl sits in a chair and does a *lot* of cussing.

4. Repeat. ★½

Star Peaces (dir. G. Gaines and E. Jackson, 2007). It's the year 2007 on planet Earth, not the future, and although he has an awesome name, Luke Crazy Bad-Ass is the lamest guy in his entire neighborhood. For example: His wallet contains nothing but pudding, and instead of wanting to make out with him, girls prefer to punch him in the stomach. Then he discovers two robots in a sandbox who tell him that he can move things with his mind. There is no evidence that this is true, but he tells everyone about it anyway, and when they ask him for a demonstration, he gets really angry and does the Robot Dance of Anger. At one point, he thinks that his bike is some kind of futuristic speeder and uses it to ride around Frick Park with a Super Soaker, making space noises with his lips and attacking people that he thinks are storm troopers. Then the police show up, as in, real policemen who were not in the script but who were called up by an old lady we almost ran over. This turned out to be awesome, because we hadn't really written an ending. ★★½

Hello, Good-Die (dir. G. Gaines and E. Jackson, 2008). Breakthrough! This was the first of many of our films to use sock puppets. James Bondage, British superspy, wakes up in bed with a beautiful woman, who is secretly a sock puppet. We know that it's a secret from when James Bondage says, "The most beautiful thing about you is that you're not a sock puppet." ★★½

Cat-ablanca (dir. G. Gaines and E. Jackson, 2008). The thing is, cats can't act. ★

2002 (dir. G. Gaines and E. Jackson, 2009). We felt very liberated after watching *2001*. If *Aguirre, the Wrath of God* taught us that the plot of a film doesn't need to have a happy ending, *2001* taught us that a film doesn't even need a plot in the first place, and a lot of its scenes can just be weird colors. Artistically, this is our most ambitious film, which also makes it the least fun to watch. ★★½

The Manchurian Cat-idate (dir. G. Gaines and E. Jackson, 2010). Not only can cats not act, they also hate wearing clothes. ★★★½

Chapter 16

HOPEFULLY THE END OF WHAT HAS BEEN A RIDICULOUS AMOUNT OF EARL BACKSTORY

All in all we made forty-two films, starting with *Earl, the Wrath of God II*. We had a ritual for when each film was finished: We would burn the film to two DVDs, erase the film on Dad's computer, and then I would take the raw footage out to the garbage behind our house while Earl smoked a cigarette. Mom usually watched disapprovingly while this happened—she thought we would want the footage for later, and also, while she tolerated the smoking, at the same time she wasn't exactly the biggest fan—but she let us do it, because we didn't give her a choice.

We didn't want anyone watching the films but us. No one. Not Mom and Dad; we knew we couldn't trust their opinions. Not our classmates; we didn't *care* about their opinions, not after the *Aguirre, the Wrath of God* fiasco. Also, it's not like we really were friends with any of them.

In Earl's case, the fact is that he just didn't give a shit about making friends. I was the closest friend he had, and aside from making films, we didn't hang out all that much. In middle school he started spending a lot of time on his own; I didn't know where he went, but it wasn't his house or mine. There was a period where he was doing drugs, but I wasn't really privy to any of that. It didn't last very long, either; there were two movies that we did where he was sort of cracked out the whole time (*Walk Lola Walk* [2008], *Gay.I.* [2008]), and then pretty quickly he got himself together. By eighth grade, he had restricted himself to cigarettes. However, he remained a very solitary person, and there were weeks where I didn't see him at all.

And as for me: In middle school I just had a hard time making friends. I don't know why. If I knew why, it wouldn't have been so impossible. One thing was that I just usually wasn't interested in what other kids were interested in. For a lot of kids, it was sports or music, two things that I just couldn't really get into. Music really only interested me as a soundtrack to a movie, and as for sports, I mean, come on. It's some guys throwing some balls around, or trying to knock each other over, and you're supposed to watch them for three hours at a time, and it just sort of seems like a waste. I dunno. I don't want to sound condescending, so I'm not going to say anything else, except that it is literally impossible to imagine a thing dumber than sports.

So I didn't really share any interests with anyone. More to the point, I'd be in some kind of social situation, and I had no idea what to talk about. I definitely didn't know how to make jokes that weren't part of a movie, and so instead I would freak out and try to think of the most interesting possible thing to say, and it was usually something like:

1. Have you ever noticed that people look like either rodents or

birds? And you can classify them that way, like, I definitely have more of a rodent face, but you look like a penguin.

2. If this were a video game, you could just break everything in this room and a bunch of money would come out of it, and you wouldn't even have to pick it up, you would just walk into it and suddenly it would be in your bank account.

3. If I were to talk like the lead singer of some old-school rock band, like for example Pearl Jam, everyone would think I literally had a severe head injury. So how come the guy from Pearl Jam was allowed to do it?

These are all great things to talk about when you're friends with someone, but not when you're just trying to make polite conversation. And somehow I just never got to the friendship stage. By the time I got to high school, and figured out how to talk to other people a little better, I had decided I didn't really *want* to be friends with anyone. Other than Earl, who like I said was really more of a coworker.

And girls? Forget about girls. There was never any chance, with girls. For reference, please refer to chapter 3, "Let's Just Get This Embarrassing Chapter Out of the Way."

So, to conclude, we never showed the films to anyone.

Chapter 17

MR. McCARTHY'S OFFICE

Mr. McCarthy is one of the only reasonable teachers at Benson. He's on the young side and seems somehow immune to the life-crushing qualities of high school. Many of the young teachers at Benson cry at least once a day; a few others are just sort of dumb and tyrannical, in the conventional mold; but Mr. McCarthy is his own kind of guy.

He's white, but he has a shaved head, and his forearms are covered in tattoos. Nothing gets him more fired up than facts. If anyone in class cites a fact of any kind, he pounds his chest and yells, "TRUE FACT," or sometimes, "RESPECT THE RESEARCH." If the fact is wrong, this becomes "FALSE FACT." He drinks Vietnamese soup out of a thermos, all day, and he refers to drinking soup as "consulting the oracle." On rare occasions when he gets really excited, he pretends to be a dog. Most of the time he's insanely easygoing, and sometimes he teaches barefoot.

Anyway, Mr. McCarthy is the only teacher I have anything close to a kind of friendship with, and he lets me and Earl eat lunch in his office.

Earl is always morose during this time. He takes remedial courses, and his classmates are nitwits. Also, all remedial classrooms are on the B floor, which is below the surface of the earth.

By the way, Earl is smart enough to place into any classes he wants. I have no idea why he takes remedial courses, and Earl's decision making is a thing that would need like twenty books to explore, so I'm not going into it here. The point is that by seventh period, he's been exposed to four hours of grinding stupidity, and he wants to slit his wrists. For the first ten minutes of lunch, he shakes his head angrily at everything I say. Then eventually he snaps out of it.

"So you been spending time with this girl now," he said the day after my ill-advised lunch in the cafeteria.

"Yeah."

"Your mom still making you."

"Pretty much, yeah."

"She gonna die or what."

"Uhhh," I said. I didn't really know what to say about this. "I mean, she's got cancer. But *she* doesn't think she's gonna die, so I feel sort of bad when we're hanging out, because the whole time I'm thinking, you're gonna die you're gonna die you're gonna die."

Earl was stony-faced. "Everybody dies," he said. Actually, he said "Irrybody dies," but that looks stupid written out somehow. How does writing even work? I hate this.

"Yeah," I said.

"You believe in the afterlife?"

"Not really."

"Nuh, you do." Earl sounded pretty sure about this.

"No, I don't."

"You can't *not* believe in no afterlife."

"That's uh—that's a triple negative," I said, to be annoying. Which was stupid because you shouldn't *practice* being annoying.

"Man, fuck you. Think you're too good for the afterlife."

We ate. Earl's lunch was Skittles, SunChips, cookies, and Coke. I was eating some of his cookies. "You can't wrap your head around *not* living. You can't actually believe that you're not gonna be alive."

"I have a very powerful brain."

"I'm bout to kick that brain in the head," said Earl, stomping the ground a little bit for no reason.

Mr. McCarthy entered.

"Greg. Earl."

"Sup, Mr. McCarthy."

"Earl, that lunch is garbage." Mr. McCarthy was maybe one of four people in the world who could say this to Earl without him freaking out.

"Least I ain't drinkin no funky seaweed-lookin . . . *tentacle soup* out of no thermos."

For some reason Earl and I were both obsessed with tentacles during this time.

"Yeah, I was just coming in here to replenish the oracle."

That was when we noticed the hot plate on his desk.

"They're rewiring the teachers' lounge," explained Mr.

McCarthy. "This, my boys, is the source of all wisdom. Gaze into the waters of the oracle."

We looked into Mr. McCarthy's huge vat of soup. Earl's description was pretty much on the money; the noodles looked like tentacles, and there were a lot of soggy wispy green leafy things. Actually, it looked like an entire ecosystem in there. I was sort of expecting to see snails.

"It's called *pho*," said Mr. McCarthy. "Pho" is apparently pronounced "fuh."

"Lemme try some," said Earl.

"Nope," said Mr. McCarthy.

"Dag," said Earl.

"Can't give you guys food," apologized Mr. McCarthy. "It's one of those things they really don't like teachers doing. It's a shame. Earl, I can recommend a particular Vietnamese restaurant for you if you want. Thuyen's Saigon Flavor, over in Lawrenceville."

"I ain't eatin out in no *Lawrenceville*," said Earl with disdain.

"Earl refuses to go to Lawrenceville," I said. I found that sometimes with Earl and another person around, a fun thing to do was narrate Earl's behavior, especially if it meant simply rephrasing things that he said. Basically, the premise was that he had some irritating personal assistant who actually wasn't useful in any way.

"I ain't got eatin-out *money.*"

"Earl has no money allocated for that purpose."

"Tryna get some *soup* up in here."

"Earl was hoping to have some of *your* soup."

"Not gonna happen," announced Mr. McCarthy cheerfully, closing the tureen of soup. "Greg, throw me a fact."

"Uh . . . Like much Vietnamese cuisine, pho includes elements of French cooking, specifically the broth, which is derived from the consommé." I'm embarrassed to say this, but that fact came from the Food Network.

"RESPECT THE RESEARCH," barked Mr. McCarthy. "Greg, you beasted on that fact." He flexed his right biceps, then punched it with his left fist. "Continue the dominance." He was insanely fired up. He was actually snarling a little. I thought he was going to attack me. Instead, he turned to face Earl.

"Earl, if you change your mind, you can tell Thuyen to put it on Mr. McCarthy's tab. All right?"

"Awright."

"His pho is much better than mine anyway."

"Awright."

"Gentlemen."

"Mr. McCarthy."

As soon as Mr. McCarthy left, of course, we got some paper cups and macked on that soup. It tasted OK: like chicken soup, but with strange overtones that we couldn't identify. Sort of garlicky and licoricey at the same time. Anyway, it wasn't mind-blowing. At least, not at first.

I first started to feel funny when the bell rang at the end of the day. I stood up and all the blood rushed to my head and I got that brown fuzzy wall in front of my eyes that you sometimes get when the blood rushes to your head, and I had to stand

there until it went away. Meanwhile, my eyes were still open, and apparently they were staring at Liv Ryan, the first girl at our school to get a nose job. Specifically, my eyes were staring at her boobs.

From behind the brown fuzzy wall, Liv said some words. I could definitely hear the words, but for some reason I wasn't able to put them together.

I had no idea what the fuck was going on.

"Greg, what's your *problem*," said Liv again, and this time I was able to determine what she was saying, and also her boobs slowly materialized.

"Blood," I said. "My, uh, head."

"What," she said.

"Couldn't see," I said. It was hard to talk. Also, I had become aware that I looked and sounded like a moron. My voice sounded ridiculously nasal, like my face was about 80 percent nose.

"Blood rushed to my head and I couldn't see," I explained, although I may not have said all of those words correctly, or in that order.

"Greg, you don't look so good," someone else said.

"Can you just not look at me, please," said Liv, and her words filled my heart with terror.

"I have to go," I blurted. I realized that I needed to get my bag, and moved my feet for some reason.

That is when I fell down.

I probably don't need to tell you that nothing is funnier at Benson, or any other high school, than when a human being falls down. I don't mean witty, or legitimately funny; I'm just saying, people in high school think falling down is the funniest thing that a person can possibly do. I'm not sure why this is true, but it is. People completely lose control when they see this happen. Sometimes they *themselves* fall down, and then the entire world collapses on itself.

So I fell down. Normally, I would have been able to deal with it by getting up and bowing, or doing an ironic celebration or something. However, I wasn't feeling normal. I couldn't think straight. "Everyone is laughing at you," my brain was telling me, instead of providing me with valuable information, or coming up with a plan. "It's because you fell down like an idiot!" My brain was malfunctioning. I panicked. I grabbed my bag and actually lunged for the door, and in the process, *fell down a second time.*

People were close to throwing up from laughing so hard. It was truly a gift from the Comedy Gods: a chubby guy falling down, freaking out, lurching in the direction of the door, and falling down again.

Meanwhile, I scrambled out the door and into the hall, and somehow the hall was about three times longer than normal and just totally packed with people. I was swimming in a sea of human flesh, and trying not to completely freak out. Faces floated past and they all seemed to be staring at me. I was trying to be invisible, but I have never felt so conspicuous in my entire life. I was the Human Nose, as well as Fall-Down Boy.

It was probably five minutes, but it seemed like it took an hour to get outside, and it was an hour of hell. Then, as soon as I was through the school doors and onto the front steps, I got a text.

that soup had drugs .meet me in parking lot

It was Earl.

"McCarthy puts weed in that soup," he hissed. This took a while to register with me.

"Man, he musta put a damn ton of weed in there," continued Earl. "Cuz I didn't even have that much. You had seconds, though. You must be *done*, son."

"Yeah," I said.

"You look high *as hell*."

"I fell down."

"Damn," said Earl. "Wish I'd seen that."

So this was what it was like to get high. I had tried smoking marijuana once before at a party thrown by Dave Smeggers, but nothing happened. Maybe I hadn't been smoking it right.

"Let's go to your house and mack on some grub," suggested Earl.

"OK," I said, and we started walking. But actually, the more I thought about it, that sounded like a terrible idea. I looked high as hell! According to Earl! So when we got home: Mom and Dad would immediately know that I was on drugs! Fuck! Then we would have to talk about it! I wasn't capable of talking about anything! I wasn't really even capable of thinking with words! I had this badger image in my head for some reason! *That badger was awesome!*

Also, I would have to make something up because I didn't want to get Mr. McCarthy in trouble. What was I going to say? That some random stoner kids *forced* us to get high? That was ridiculous, right? Where the hell was I supposed to tell them we had gotten high from? And maybe more importantly: *How was I going to make it all the way to the bus without falling down again?*

"Do McCarthy act stoned in class," asked Earl. "Cuz this is lights out. I can't wait to get my *grub* on. Damn."

Earl was in an awesome mood. I was not. In addition to worrying about Mom and Dad, I felt that everyone on the street was staring at us with disapproval. We were two kids on drugs, just walking around! We were incredibly high! And my nose was like a blimp attached to my face! A blimp filled with mucus! How could we *not* be the center of attention? (Only in retrospect did I realize that, on the Can't Stop Watching Scale of Interestingness, me and Earl walking down the street does not get a very high rating. [Ha ha! "High" rating! Get it? That's truly hilarious. Just kidding, of course; that joke sucked. In fact, that type of joke is the reason most people hate stoners.])

"Do McCarthy act all *stoned*," repeated Earl. "While he teaching."

"He—not really," I said. "Well, maybe. Sort of. I guess. You could, uh . . . Not exactly, uh. You know."

I couldn't even put a goddamned sentence together.

Earl was temporarily silenced by this display.

"Damn, son," he said eventually. "Damn."

While we were on the bus to my house, I got another text.

going in for chemo tomw. do u want 2 say goodbye 2 my hair? :)

I'm embarrassed to say that it took us the entire bus ride to decipher this message. First of all, we did not understand that "chemo tomw" were abbreviations. Instead, we thought they were nonsense words. We said them to each other.

"Tcheh-moe tom-wah."

"Khee-moo tuh-moe."

"Emu tomb."

"Ha . . . ha . . . ha."

"Heh heh."

"No seriously, what, uh."

"Heh."

"Harf."

Finally, as we were leaving the bus, Earl figured it out. "Chemotherapy," he said.

"Ohhhh."

"Your girl gonna lose all her hair."

"What?"

"Chemotherapy. You get injected with a shitload of chemicals and all your hair fall out."

This struck me as ridiculous, even though I sort of knew it was true. "Ohhhhh."

"You basically get sick as hell."

Well, I thought to myself, this is a pretty pickle. Then I started thinking about the phrase "pretty pickle." Pretty soon I was envisioning a cucumber with Madison Hartner's face and boobs. Somehow this was hilarious.

"Dude," said Earl, who looked concerned.

"What?"

"Why you laughing."

"Uhhh."

"Chemotherapy is serious. You don't want to be cracking up about no chemotherapy."

"No, it was, uh . . . I was thinking about something else." Jesus Christ, I was a mess.

"So you gonna text her back, tell her we're coming."

I wasn't sure if this was a question. "Maybe?"

"Yeah, we gotta see your friend, dumbass."

"OK. OK."

"So write, yeah, me and Earl gonna come see you."

This took forever to write, and I ended up with:

oaky sounds grea8~! but can i bring frined earl hes cool ul'l liek him ???/

Holy flame-throwing Jesuses. There are definitely kids out there who enjoy being on drugs, but I can promise you that Greg Gaines is not one of them.

Chapter 18

DRUGS ARE THE WORST

Our first obstacle was Denise.

"Hello, Greg," she said. She seemed preoccupied. She was also giving Earl the crazy eye, sort of like if I had showed up on her doorstep with a llama. "And who might this be?"

Earl and I said something at the same time.

"Sorry?"

Then neither of us said anything.

"I'm Denise," said Denise eventually.

"Earl Jackson," said Earl, too loudly. I eyed him fearfully. When talking with adults, Earl often becomes brash and combative. I knew this was not going to go over well with Denise, so I started talking. This turned out to be a tactical error.

What not-on-drugs Greg would have said: "Earl's a good friend of mine, and he wanted to wish Rachel well. Is she upstairs?"

What on-drugs Greg ended up saying: "Earl's my best—Earl's one of my best friends. And we were just hanging out together, you know, like, not really doing anything, you know, so it's cool.

So, uh. So we got this text, from Rachel, about the hair loss—which, I mean, hasn't happened yet, obviously, so we wanted to see her hair. And hang out! Not just see the hair, because, you know, the hair, I can take it or leave it. I'm sure she's gonna look great without hair. But we just wanted to hang out. Say what's up, that sort of . . . thing."

By the end of this monologue I was covered in sweat. Meanwhile, Earl was not even trying to hide his disgust. He had his face in his hands and said a word that I think was "Goddamn."

"Oka-a-a-ay," said Denise, sounding uncertain.

We were all silent for a while.

"So is Rachel upstairs?" I said eventually.

"Yeah, yeah, of course," said Denise and waved us up, and we ran up there and away from Denise with extreme quickness.

Our second obstacle was Rachel's mistrust of Earl, and also our record-setting drug-related weirdness.

"I wasn't sure what your text message meant," she said. She was eyeing Earl warily. I had the queasy feeling that she was mistrustful of him because he was black, although I also felt terrible for thinking that, because that would be accusing a girl of racism who is about to lose all her hair, and then probably die.

"Earl's the man," I said, as if this explained anything.

"Yeah, you guys send gross text messages to each other."

It took me a long, uncomfortably silent time to remember that this was the only thing I had ever said to Rachel about

Earl, and by the time I remembered that, Earl had already taken some initiative.

"Sup."

"Hello, Earl."

Silence.

"I like your room."

"Thank you. Greg thinks it's too girly."

I knew I had to say something here, so I sort of yelled, "I do not!"

"Of course it's girly," said Earl. "*My* room doesn't have no James Bond in no . . . *thong.*"

What not-on-drugs Greg would have said: "Yeah, Earl prefers his James Bond posters naked."

What on-drugs Greg ended up saying: "Huh huh."

Longer silence.

"So, I'm getting a round of chemo tomorrow."

"Yeah, that sucks."

"Dude, what the hell." Earl shoved me.

"What?"

"Don't say it sucks."

"Uh . . . yeah, you're right."

"It sucks a little bit," said Rachel.

"Yeah, but it's exciting."

"I guess."

"If you get it early enough, you've got a good chance," said Earl, staring at the ground.

"Yup." Rachel was also staring at the ground.

Possibly racist silence.

Rachel and Earl were clearly not hitting it off. I had to do something. Unfortunately, I had no idea what that thing would be. The silence grew. Rachel continued staring at the ground. Earl started sighing. It was the opposite of a party. It was about the least fun social situation imaginable. If terrorists had burst into the room and tried to suffocate us in hummus, it would have been an improvement. This idea got me thinking about hummus. What is hummus, exactly? It's basically a paste. Who eats paste? Especially a paste that resembles cat barf? You can't deny the resemblance here. At least, when Cat Stevens barfs, it looks like hummus.

And then a part of me was like: "Why do you keep comparing food to barf? First the alien thing in the cafeteria, and now this. Maybe you have a problem."

That's when I realized that I was giggling. But sort of in a nervous scared way, which made it even more obnoxious than just lighthearted giggling.

Earl was pissed: "Stop it with your goddamn giggling." But Rachel's reaction was worse: "You guys can go if you want," she said, and it sounded like she was about to cry. This was terrible. I felt like such a dickhead. It was time to come clean.

"We're on drugs," I blurted.

Earl had his head in his hands again.

"What?" said Rachel.

"We accidentally got high."

"Accidentally?"

It was time to come *sort of* clean. Actually, it was high time for Lie Time.

"I totally blacked out. I don't even remember what happened."

"You did *not* black out," snapped Earl.

"No, we both did."

"The hell are you even *talkin* about."

"Why are you guys on drugs?" asked Rachel.

"I don't know!" I said. "I *don't know.*"

Then Earl started to say something, and I knew it was going to be about Mr. McCarthy. But I really didn't want to get him fired.

So I just started talking: "Actually, we went into a bathroom, and there were some guys there, you know, some of the stoner guys, and they were like, you want some weed, and at first we were like, no, we don't want any of your, uh, weed, but then they started getting angry, and were like, yo, you better smoke some of this, or we'll, uh, beat the hell out of you, and there were like twenty of them, so we were like, OK fine, so we smoked with them, but again, I don't totally remember what happened because I blacked out."

Immediately Obvious Holes in the Story That I Just Made Up: A Partial List

1. Earl and I have never visited a bathroom together in our entire lives, probably because that would be weird.

2. Stoners do not smoke weed in the bathroom. They smoke weed in old Nissan Altimas about a block and a half from the school. Then they are not seen again for hours, sometimes days.

3. No stoner in the history of the world has ever forced anyone to smoke with them. Indeed, many of them are actually delighted *not* to share weed with you.

4. There were *twenty* of them? In one bathroom? Twenty stoners? Why not just say a hundred? Why not say a berjillion? Jesus.

5. What is this "blacking out" business? What would that even mean?

So I said all that, and Earl was silent. Rachel looked at him for confirmation. At length he said: "Yeah, that's what happened." He was pissed.

We looked like morons. But at least Rachel wasn't on the verge of crying anymore. She looked sort of amused.

"I *hate* drugs," I said. "I feel like an ass right now. I'm sorry we came over while we were on drugs."

"Shut your dumb ass up," said Earl to me. "You think you're making Rachel feel better? All apologetic and shit? Shut the hell up."

"OK," I said.

"Rachel," continued Earl, who was now in Take-Control Mode, to my vast relief, because when Earl takes control, good things happen. "We came over here to wish you well and cheer you up. So let's go walk around and get ice cream or something."

Holy shit, this was such a good idea. I told you Earl always has the best ideas.

Chapter 19

EARL BETRAYS OUR ENTIRE CREATIVE PARTNERSHIP WHILE I AM DISTRACTED BY THE MUNCHIES

Like I said, once Rachel found out we were on drugs, she was more amused than anything else.

"Greg, I didn't know you were such a bad-ass," she said.

"I'm not."

"I was being sarcastic."

"Oh."

We were at this ridiculously good ice-cream-and-waffles place in Shadyside where they mix things into your ice cream with a blender or something. The ice cream itself is unbelievable. The list of things that they mix into the ice cream, moreover, is insane. Example: bee pollen. Second example: habanero peppers. Did I get both of those? Yes. Did I have them in the weirdest flavor of ice cream available, namely, Kahlúa? The answer to your question is on board the S.S. *Yes*. When I ordered bee pollen, was I actually thinking of honey? Perhaps the actress Yessica Alba can answer that for you.

Anyway, I lost all control when I got my ice cream, and I spent five minutes completely oblivious to the outside world, because oh my God was that ice cream delicious. When I emerged, everything had changed, and also a lot of parts of my body were sticky. For example: both ankles. Earl had trouble dealing with this.

"Dude. You gotta learn . . . not to eat . . . like that."

"Mmmh sorry."

"That was so nasty," said Earl, unable to eat his own ice cream. "Dag."

"Mmmnh kinda want another one," I said.

"You should get one," suggested Rachel.

"Naw. He shouldn't."

"Mmmngh."

"We should get back anyway," said Earl, shouldering his backpack. "If we gonna watch something before dinner."

"Nnnh yeah? What are we watching?"

Earl and Rachel stared at me.

"Dude."

"Greg, we were going to watch a few of the films you guys made." Rachel said this like it wasn't a big deal.

"Did you not even hear us or some shit?" asked Earl.

"Uh."

"Dag."

From nowhere, Earl produced a lit cigarette and angrily started puffing on it. Meanwhile, I think Rachel was sensing that I was freaking out. "Greg, Earl said it would be fine—do you really not want me to see what you've worked so hard on?"

The answer to *that* question was locked in a vault deep within the hull of the Starship *Holy Fuck Definitely Not.*

Jesse Andrews

Ideally, I would have been able to take Earl aside and make these points:

I. What the hell are you doing.
    A. Did you just offer to show Rachel our films?
        1. That seems to be what happened, while I was eating ice cream.
        2. Correct me if I'm wrong.
    B. The films that we long ago agreed never to show anyone?
        1. They're not good enough to show people.
        2. Maybe someday we'll make something worth showing to people.
        3. But we're definitely not there yet.
    C. Fuckfuckfuckfuck. *Dicksmuggler.*
II. Why the hell are you doing this?
    A. Is it because she's dying?
        1. That shouldn't have anything to do with anything.
        2. Goddammit! *Earl.*
    B. Or maybe you've just changed your mind about whether or not our films are good?
        1. Because, they're not.
        2. Right?
        3. We don't have a budget or good lighting or anything.
        4. We're just fucking around in a lot of them!
        5. We're basically morons.
III. Earl, you jackass.
    A. You're really being a douche right now.
    B. A huge douche.

C. Please don't windmill-kick me in the head.
    1. OW
    2. FUCK

But I wasn't able to say any of that. Instead, I just sort of nodded and went along with it. It was two against one anyway. I didn't really have a choice.

We walked home. On the bright side, I was starting to feel like myself again, but it didn't really compensate for the total betrayal of Earl, and the humiliation that we were both about to endure. I guess it goes to show that being around a dying girl will make some people do anything. Even foul-tempered, height-challenged filmmakers.

Chapter 20

BATMAN VERSUS SPIDER-MAN

Batman versus Spider-Man (dir. G. Gaines and E. Jackson, 2011). Batman loves bats; Spider-Man loves spiders. Batman is wearing a bunch of extra clothes under his suit so as to appear more muscular; Spider-Man is fast and wiry, or at least, more twitchy. The bat and the spider have never been enemies . . . *until now!!!* Actually, they're still not enemies. A movie producer locked them in a room together and won't let them out until one of them has been vanquished, but they don't feel like fighting each other. Mostly they sit around having painful weapons malfunctions. ★★★½

Critical response to *Batman versus Spider-Man* was positive, more so than we expected. Although, to be honest, the reviewer was a total pushover. She laughed pretty much nonstop throughout the entire thing, and wasn't taking any notes. She probably didn't notice the mediocre lighting and frequent shadow problems, for example. Or the numerous costuming inconsistencies, like how my copious sweating kept undoing the Batman horns that I made in my hair with mousse.

So, yeah. It was weird watching one of our films with someone else. For the first two or three minutes I was talking nonstop, explaining everything:

"OK, so this is just a shot of some cartoons that we drew, because we were trying to do that thing in comic-book movies where they—wait, it'll come back into focus—yeah, so they start out by showing pictures from actual comic books—and now, yeah, Earl is chewing on it, because, I dunno. And now he's freaking out. OK. So the stick figure on the left is Batman, and if you look closely, we sort of screwed it up, but if you look at the right moment you can kind of see that he has, um, stick junk. Uh, junk, like genitalia. OK, and on the right Spider-Man is eating a waffle, which later becomes important becaus—"

Then Earl told me to shut up.

So I was sitting there silently taking note of everything that was going wrong while Rachel emitted a constant stream of giggling and snorting, with occasional eruptions, like a human mud pot. It was a strange experience. I didn't know what to make of it. I think mainly it confirmed my suspicion that if you've made a film, you can't watch it with anyone you know, because their opinions are going to be biased and worthless. I mean, it was nice to make something that cracked someone else up. But would Rachel have thought the film was hilarious if Earl and I were total strangers? Doubtful.

So really this was just a confirmation that showing our films

to people was a mistake. But we ended up paying a pretty heavy price for it.

                    EARL
        You got them steak tips still?

                    ME
        No, I ate those a couple days ago.

                    EARL
        Dammit.

Chapter 21

TWO PONCY DUDES

And the next day, Rachel went off to the hospital to get shot full of drugs and radioactive particles and whatnot. *Little did I know that I would soon be joining her in the very same hospital.*

Actually, what the hell is this "little did I know" business. I didn't know at *all* that I would soon be joining her in the very same hospital, because I can't see into the goddamned *future*. Why would I be able to know that even a little? "Little did I know." Jesus.

You can take pretty much any sentence in this book and if you read it enough times, you will probably end up committing a homicide.

So Rachel was in the hospital, and Earl and I were at home watching *Withnail and I*, an obscure British film about two actors who are constantly drunk and on drugs. They take an insane vacation in the countryside, where they almost starve to death. Then the uncle of one of the actors shows up and basically tries to have sex with the other one. We were just getting ready to do a

new film, but we hadn't gotten *Mulholland Drive* in the mail yet, so we found *Withnail and I* in Dad's collection and it was good enough that we were debating doing a remake of it.

It was actually sort of awesome. The constant alcohol-related freaking out of Withnail reminded us a lot of Klaus Kinski in *Aguirre, the Wrath of God*, and we were fired up that there were accents that we could try to do. In general, I would say Earl is slightly better than me at accents, but that doesn't mean he's actually any good at all.

"How does he say it? The Irish man in the bar? 'I—Aye cahlled him a ponce.'"

"Naw. He say it like, 'OI CARLLED HEM A PON—A PORNCE.'"

"Ha!"

"PAWWWWRNCE."

"Oh man. That's not it, but that's a lot funnier."

The word "ponce" kind of dominated one of the scenes. It turns out it's British slang for "child molester." We thought it was a little fucked up that they had a slang word for that, but then Earl pointed out that in America we say "motherfucker" all the time, which is just as disturbing.

"It fyeels like a pyig shat in my head."

"HOW SHID OI KNOW WHERRRE WE AHRE? ET FEELS LOIKE A PEG SHAT IN ME EDD."

"I think that's a different British accent."

"Yeah. It's the one from *Fish Tank*."

Fish Tank is an obscure recent movie we saw about an insane

English girl from the projects. We loved that movie. We gave it an A for accents, A+ for profanity.

"So in this remake—"

"We gotta have 'ponce' in the title."

"Yeah. That's a good idea. We could call it *Poncy Scheme.*"

"The fuck's that mean."

"It's like, a play on Ponzi scheme. Like the whole Madoff thing that happened a few years ago."

"The fuck you talking about right now."

"It's fine. Never mind."

"This title don't have to be all clever and shit. We could just call it *Two Poncy Dudes.*"

"Actually that's not bad!"

"*Ponce-Ass Dudes on Vacation.* Simple as hell."

"That's perfect. So I think you should be Withnail."

"Withnearl."

"Yeah. So I think the plot is pretty straightforward. Most of the time you're drinking and then freaking out."

"Lighter fluid and shit."

"Yeah, that scene is going to be awesome."

"I'm also gonna be that gay uncle. Draw a fake mustache and pretend to be all fat and shit. Be like, Boy, I'm gay as hell. I'ma fuck you."

At the end of the movie, Withnail is bellowing at some wolves in the zoo. This scene was on our minds for some reason, so we decided to shoot it first. However, we didn't have access to wolves. Instead, we decided that Earl should try bellowing at

Doopie, the Jacksons' big terrifying dog. This meant we had to go to Earl's house.

"Maybe when we done with this we should visit Rachel at the hospital," Earl commented as we got on our bikes.

"Oh," I said. "Yeah. I don't know if today's OK to visit or when visiting hours are or whatever."

"I called em," said Earl. "We can show up anytime before seven."

This was sort of surprising to me, and I was thinking about it on the ride to Earl's. I mean, deep down, Earl is obviously a much better person than I am. But I still didn't expect him to go to the trouble of calling the hospital for visiting hours and stuff. I guess it's not really that hard to make a five-minute phone call, but it still struck me as something I wouldn't have done unless someone made me do it.

Then I continued thinking about it and I got kind of depressed that I don't even have my shit enough together to call the hospital and figure out when I can go visit. I really needed to step it up, or I was going to be the worst friend in the history of dying girls.

Basically I was thinking, thank God for Earl. Because I don't really have a moral compass and I need to rely on him for guidance, or else I might accidentally become like a hermit or a terrorist or something. How fucked up is that? Am I even a human? Who the hell knows.

INT. JACKSON LIVING ROOM — LATE AFTERNOON

                    MAXWELL
Roll your damn pants down.

                     EARL
I biked over here.

                    MAXWELL
No one wants to see your weird-ass
socks.

                     EARL
Nobody care about my socks.

                    MAXWELL
                  angrily
No one wants to see them *nasty socks.*

On our way in, we stumbled into Maxwell, one of Earl's half brothers. Earl had his pant legs rolled up. This caused Maxwell to become enraged.

If you are confused as to why this would cause Maxwell to become enraged, that is totally understandable. I've learned over the years that basically anything can get anyone in the Jackson house enraged.

Cause: Madden '08 disc is scratched

Effect: Maxwell hurls Brandon into the television

Cause: Humidity

Effect: Felix uses Derrick's forehead to inflict damage on
Devin's face

Cause: There is a bird outside

Effect: Brandon strides around aiming blows
indiscriminately at people's testicles

When a fight breaks out, everyone is fair game, and
unfortunately that includes the doughy, slow-moving white
kid. As a result, my reflexes at Chez Jackson have become pretty
quick. The moment someone takes off their shoe to hit someone
else in the face, or someone else has their elbow in another kid's
mouth, I am halfway out the exit. If we're not near an exit, I
try to hide behind some furniture, although then when it gets
shoved into a wall, sometimes I become part of that wall.

Anyway, Maxwell put Earl in a headlock and punched his
head while Earl thrashed around. The commotion attracted the
attention of several brothers, including Brandon, the thirteen-
year-old psychopath with the "TRU NIGGA" neck tattoo. He
came hurtling down the stairs like a missile with elbows. His
teeth were bared, and his eyes were locked on mine. I made a
small shrieking noise and turned to run.

Maxwell and Earl were in Brandon's way, so I actually did
make it out of the door before Brandon was able to elbow me
in the head. The problem is, I got too excited. When I got to
the end of the porch, instead of jumping, I sort of dove, as in,
headfirst.

There's a convention in films where, when someone is flying

through the air, time slows down. The person gets to observe all of the various details of their environment, reconsider their course of action, maybe even contemplate the notion of God. Anyway, this convention is a lie. If anything, time *sped up.* My feet left the porch and immediately I was lying all scraped up on some cement with a broken arm. Almost as immediately, Brandon was standing over me.

"Yeah, nigga," he piped, in his not-all-the-way-dropped thirteen-year-old voice. "Yeah, clumsy bitch." He kicked me kind of halfheartedly.

"OW," I said. This angered him. He kicked me harder.

"Shut the hell up," he said, but the second kick actually hurt a lot, so I began screaming. This made Brandon slap my face repeatedly. Fortunately, Felix had just arrived on the scene, and according to his own mysterious logic, his reaction to what he saw was to grab Brandon by the head and throw him across the yard.

He turned to me. We stared at each other. His eyes were cold with disgust.

Eventually, he said: "Fuck outta here," and walked back into the house.

Chapter 22

SPIDER VERSUS WASP

So, that was how I came to be in the same hospital as Rachel. Although it was a completely different wing of the hospital—hers was the chemotherapy area, and mine was the broken-arm-that-had-somehow-become-infected area. No one seemed to know how my broken arm got infected. Pretty quickly I stopped asking about it. I was worried I would find out that there were other basic medical facts that the nurses didn't know, like where skin comes from, or how surgery works.

But yeah, my broken arm got infected, and I ran a fever, and all of that meant a lengthy stay in the hospital. And that meant visitors. Each of these visitors had various points to make.

Mom
- Poor, poor sweetie.
- We're gonna get you out of here soon.
- Oh, my poor brave boy.
- You must be so bored.
- Here are some books that I collected at random from your

room or the library.

- I'll just put these books on top of those other books from last time.
- You have to make sure to do your schoolwork.
- You have to make sure to tell the nurses if *anything* feels funny.
- If you have even the slightest headache, you need to get on the phone and call the nurses *right away because it might be meningitis.*
- I said *it might be meningitis.*
- Meningitis is a fatal brain disease, and in hospitals you're sometimes more vulnerable to—
- You know what, I don't want to scare you with this.
- Just if you have even the tiniest headache, call the nurses.
- I'm just being crazy, but seriously, call them.
- Does your phone work?
- Let me just see if it works.

Mom accompanied by Gretchen

- We thought we'd come here and cheer you up.
- Gretchen, do you want to say anything to your brother?
- Gretchen, can you just cooperate for *fifteen minutes.*
- Gretchen. *This is not a game.*
- I can't *believe* you refuse to cooperate *even with this.*
- Just go wait outside then. You are really being awful. You are being just awful and I wish I knew why. I'll be outside in five minutes.
- Jesus.

Mom accompanied by Grace

- Grace drew you a picture!
- It's a picture of Cat Stevens!
- It's a what? Oh.
- It's a bear.
- Grace drew you a *very handsome bear.*

Earl

- sup, ike
- i talked to some a your teachers
- you gotta write an essay or some shit
- you gotta do a list of problems outta some book
- ms. harrad says don't worry about the test friday, you and her gonna talk about it when you get back, also she hope you get better
- mr. cubaly want you to do some test while you in here but i got no idea how that suppose to happen so my advice is don't worry about it
- you got *mulholland drive* in the mail from netflix so i watched it
- that shit is fucked the fuck up, no joke
- we gotta watch it once you get out of here
- that shit is crazy as hell
- lesbians and shit
- look at you
- you gonna be a weak little bitch when you get outta here
- you just lying in bed all damn day
- what else, what else

- oh i went to see your girl again
- she got a bald-ass head right now
- she look like darth vader without the helmet
- chemo is no joke, son
- she axed me for some of our films last time so i lent em to her
- i dunno which ones, i gave her like ten of em
- whoa
- what the hell are you yelling about?
- are you being serious right now? are you being serious with me right now?
- you need to calm your ass down
- you need to be *toning this shit down* right about now
- man, that girl has a damn bag full of chemicals in her body right now, she need something to cheer her the hell up, she happy as hell about these films
- i mean no she is not happy as hell but she was smiling and shit and that's a major improvement so don't be trying to bitch me out about this
- yeah, that's right, tone it down
- the fuck you think i'm gonna say no to this girl be dying out of cancer and shit.
- damn
- this is what papa gaines would call an "extenuating circumstance," am i right
- goddamn
- look
- you're being dumb as hell but i do feel you

- you know i don't like to show this shit to no one
- but you can't say no to this girl
- i do feel you, but it's like, i dunno, you do not understand how much she like our dumbass films, but she like the hell out of em
- so don't give me shit
- aight, i'm done
- feel better, son

Dad

- Well, well, well.
- You seem rather jolly today!
- No, I know. I'm just making a little joke.
- No, it can't be much fun to be in here.
- Although you do get to lead a fairly decadent lifestyle, don't you.
- With the constant television, and the food brought to you, and the mountains of books.
- Not all who stay in hospitals enjoy such luxury.
- When I was hospitalized in the Amazon, the patients were all quartered together in a single room, and instead of television, all we had to watch for entertainment were the giant hairy spiders lying in wait for prey on the thatched ceiling, maybe eight feet above our faces.
- Spiders the size of your fist.
- Fangs glistening with venom.
- They each had hundreds of little black eyes that would twinkle dimly at night.

- And how they used to battle the wasps!
- Sometimes in the darkness a wasp would strike one of them, and in their struggle they would come tumbling down onto the bed, biting and stinging and thrashing and—
- OK. OK.
- It's just something to think about.

Earl accompanied by Derrick

- sup
- 'Sup, Greg.
- derrick was like, yo, earl, do they got candy at the hospital
- Yeah I was like, if I don't get to eat candy, I go bah-serk.
- so we brought you some skittles and a couple airheads
- There was three but I ate one.
- yeah
- Yo, lemme sign your cast one time.
- if you don't like these flavors obviously you can just give em back to us
- There . . . we . . . go. HA-HA!
- god*damn* derrick what the *fuck*
- TITTIES.
- you *did not just draw* a pair of bare-ass-naked titties on greg's fucking cast
- no it ain't awright, don't be saying it's awright
- YA BURNT.
- goddammit
- we gotta go

Madison

- Hello!
- I and my boobs are in your room with you!!

Yeah. Madison Hartner visited me in the hospital. Actually, I'm gonna stop doing this stupid bullet-point thing and just describe what happened with Madison. For a while I got tired of writing the normal way, but now I'm also tired of writing the bullet-point way. We really are caught between a rock and a hard place here.

If after reading this book you come to my home and brutally murder me, I truly do not blame you.

Obviously, Madison didn't come out and say, "I am really hot and I am in your room with you," but that was the takeaway for me. I had no reason to expect her, so when she appeared in the doorway with her hair all cut short in this sexy way and she was wearing a halter top and looking like a sex goddess, for about thirty seconds I wasn't even really able to say anything. I was painfully aware that prolonged hospital exposure was causing me to achieve new and historic levels of pastiness.

"Hey, Alien Researcher."

"Huh," I said.

"I heard you got your arm broken by an alien while you were out in the field."

For a moment I had no idea what this meant, and I was worried that it was a racist comment about Earl's brothers. But this was just because I wasn't thinking clearly. I know it's an annoying stereotype that hot girls make you bad at thinking, but seriously, they do. It's like they produce nerve gas somehow. Anyway, eventually I remembered what she was talking about.

"Oh yeahhhhh."

"Oh yeah?"

"I forgot that I made that joke."

"You forgot?"

"Yeah, I got my arm broken. I was trying to collect some barf."

"Right, like you were telling us."

"Yeah, this alien was so excited to share his barf that he started whipping his tentacles around in a frenzy, and that's how it happened."

"Sounds dangerous."

"That's what true science is. It's 'extremely dangerous. But at least this space alien felt bad about it. He sent one of his alien brothers to visit me and the alien brother drew me this mystical hieroglyph on my cast. Check it out. It says, 'My heart aches with the regretful sorrow of a thousand moons,' in this really touching and beautiful alien language. Unfortunately, to us it looks like boobs."

Let's be honest: No girl is ever going to be that interested in a crude drawing of boobs. Like I said before, I can really only turn it on around less attractive girls and older women. Around hot girls, I am a mess. But Madison was giggling a little. And maybe it wasn't even out of politeness.

Then Madison said something with her beautiful lipsticky mouth that I didn't register immediately.

"Hey, I was just visiting Rachel and she was watching one of your movies."

This took a few moments to sink in. And then suddenly a section of my heart felt like it was eating itself.

"Oh. Uh . . . Yeah. Uh-huh."

"Sorry?"

"No, that's, uh, yeah. Yeahhhhhh."

"Greg, what's wrong?"

"No, it's great. Well, I mean, it's fine."

"She was really enjoying it."

"Which, um, one?"

My whole body was sweating. Like, my ears were full of sweat. Additionally, it felt like my hair was trying to uproot itself and escape from my head.

"She wouldn't tell me! She wouldn't even *show* it to me. She shut it off as soon as I walked in."

OK. This was a relief.

"Ohhh."

"She says she's not allowed to show them to anyone."

OK. Thank God. I was still freaking out—I was thinking, Madison knows that me and Earl make films, she'll inevitably tell someone about it, and soon it'll be this big weird secret thing that everyone knows—but it was also somehow comforting to have further proof that Rachel understood how I felt about the films.

"She told me that you and Earl want them to stay secret for some reason."

Rachel really did understand. That was indisputable. You had to respect that. She wasn't a filmmaker, but she had spent so much time listening to me that I guess she pretty much knew exactly how I felt about certain things, and you can't deny that it feels nice when someone knows you that well. I forced myself to relax a little bit.

"Yeah," I said. "We're pretty weird about it. I guess we're perfectionists."

Madison was quiet, but something about the way she was looking at me made me also shut up. So we both shut up for a little while. Then she said, "You have been such a good friend to Rachel. I think it's so amazing what you've been doing."

Unfortunately, this was where the Hot Girl Nerve Gas really started to take effect. Specifically, I entered Excessive Modesty Mode. Nothing is stupider and more ineffective than Excessive Modesty Mode. It is a mode in which you show that you're modest by arguing with someone who is trying to compliment you. Essentially, you are going out of your way to try to convince someone that you're a jerk.

I am the Thomas Edison of conversational stupidity.

So yeah, Madison said, "You have been such a good friend to Rachel. I think it's so amazing what you've been doing."

And obviously the best possible response for me was: "Eh. I dunno about that."

"No, you should hear the way she talks about you."

"I really can't have been that good of a friend."

"Greg, that's ridiculous."

"No, like . . . I dunno. I go to her place and just talk about myself the whole time. I'm a bad listener."

"Well, it's really cheering her up."

"It can't be cheering her up that much."

"Greg. It totally is."

"Uh, I really doubt it."

"Are you serious right now?"

"Yeah."

"Greg, *she* told *me*. That you've been an *awesome friend*."

"Well, maybe she's just lying."

"You think she's *lying*? Why would she *lie*?"

"Uhhhh."

"Greg. Oh my God. I can't believe you're arguing about this. She loves your movies, and you've given them to her, even though you won't let anyone else watch them, and that by itself is really amazing. So just shut up."

"I'm just saying."

"Why would she *lie about you being a good friend*, Greg, that's insane."

"I dunno. Girls are weird."

"No. *You're* weird."

"No, *you're weird*. I'm the only normal one."

This made Madison giggle suddenly.

"Oh my God, Greg, you're *so weird*. I love that about you, that you're so weird."

Remember what I said before? About how girls like Madison are like elephants wandering around in the undergrowth, sometimes accidentally stomping chipmunks to death and not even noticing? This is what I was talking about. Because, honestly, the rational part of me knew for a rock-solid *fact* that

I would never, ever get with Madison Hartner. But that was just the rational part of me. There's always a stupid irrational part of you, too, and you can't get rid of it. You can never completely kill off that tiny absurd spark of hope that this girl—against all odds, although she could date any guy at school, not to mention guys at college, and even though you look like the Oatmeal Monster and are a compulsive eater and suffer from constant congestion and say so many stupid things per day that it seems like a Stupid Things company is paying you to do it—this girl might like you.

And so when that girl says, "You're so weird, I love that about you," it might feel good, it might actually feel amazing, but that's just the weird chemical process that happens in your brain as you are being stomped to death by an elephant.

I think she saw that I was paralyzed, because she quickly moved on.

"Anyway, I just wanted to say, get better soon, and uh . . . I think it's awesome that you've been such a good friend to Rachel." She quickly added, "Even if you don't think so, you've made her really happy."

"I guess she likes weirdos."

"Greg, we *all* like weirdos."

My chipmunk brains and intestines were smeared all over the forest floor like pizza and Tater Tots. And the fucked-up part is, it was awesome.

Being a chipmunk is the stupidest.

Chapter 23

GILBERT

Before it was time for me to leave, I went to go visit Rachel. The cancer ward looked a lot like the part of the hospital that I had been staying in, except that the kids there were more depressing. Look. They just were. I have to be honest about this. They were paler, and weaker, and skinnier, and sicker. There was one boy—actually, it definitely could have been a girl—motionless with his eyes closed in a wheelchair, unattended by anyone, and I had to suppress what felt like a significant freak-out coming over me, because what if that boy was dead? And they just left this dead person in a wheelchair lying around? It was like, "Oh, yeah, that's Gilbert. He's been there for three days! We find that he's a helpful reminder of WHAT HAPPENS TO ALL LIVING THINGS."

Rachel looked better than most of the other kids, but she was totally bald. That really took a lot of getting used to. Every couple of minutes or so I would look at her head, or even just think about her bald head while trying not to look at it, and my skin would get all hot and prickly. As Earl pointed out, it looked a lot like Darth Vader's head when they took off his mask. It was insanely white, like it had been boiled, and sort of veiny and lumpy.

But at least she was in an OK mood—she was weak and her voice was scraggly, but she smiled when she saw me, and somehow her eyes were very happy. I don't know how to describe it. There's a chance the happiness was just from some extremely powerful pain medication they were giving her. You can never really know in a hospital.

"Yo," I said.

"The most beautiful thing about you is that you're not a sock puppet," she told me.

This was a line from *Hello, Good-Die,* our James Bond parody in which everyone is actually a sock puppet. For some reason it was hilarious that she greeted me with this line.

"Haaarf," I said.

"Thanks for visiting me."

"Yeah, I just happened to be in the neighborhood."

"Yeah, I heard."

My guard was down a little bit after the *Hello, Good-Die* thing. Usually it's when your guard is down that you find yourself saying the most dick sentences of your life. Here comes an example of that right now.

"Yeah, I thought it would be weird if I just visited you with no excuse, so I convinced Earl to break my arm so, uh, that gave me a good cover story, uhhhh. Yeah."

Jesus Christ in a cockwagon. At the beginning of this sentence, my Feeling Like a Dick Quotient was at a solid 4.0,

which is normal. By about the word "excuse," it was all the way up to 9.4. By the end I was easily maxed out at 10.0. Actually, I may have broken the scale.

Rachel was definitely not thrilled about this sentence.

"Next time maybe you can come *without* an excuse."

"Yeah, I realized that I, uh, yeah."

"Or, you don't have to come at all."

"No. What are you talking about?"

"Nothing."

"I was just making a joke."

"I know."

"Urrrrgh."

We were silent, so I made the noise again.

"Urrrrnngh."

"What is that noise."

"Regretful polar bear."

Snort.

"Polar bears are the most regretful animals in nature. Scientists do not know why this is. But they have the purest expressions of regret in the animal kingdom. Listen to how beautiful and haunting they sound: Urrrrrrrnnngh."

Snort, cough. Then Rachel said, "Actually, you shouldn't try to make me laugh."

"Oops, sorry."

"No, I like the polar bear, but when I laugh it hurts a little."

"See, now I regret doing the polar bear thing, but this feeling of regret just makes me want to make the polar bear noise even more. Because the polar bear is so regretful."

Weak snort.

"The polar bear just regrets *everything*. He *loves* fish and seals. They're his *friends*. He *hates* having to kill and eat them. But he lives too far north to go to Whole Foods, and—"

SNOORT

"Sorry, sorry. I have to chill out."

"Snnnrnn. It's OK."

"Yeah."

More silence. I inadvertently looked at Rachel's boiled-looking bald head and got the hot/prickly skin sensation for maybe the fourteenth time since arriving.

"So, how are you feeling?" I asked.

"I feel pretty good," she said. She was obviously lying. She also seemed to have decided to talk more to make me worry about her less, but talking seemed to make her kind of exhausted. "I feel kind of weak, though. I'm sorry I yelled at you when you said you needed an excuse to visit me. I just yelled at you because I'm sick."

"I totally go to town on people when I get sick."

"Yeah."

"You look good," I lied.

"No I don't," she said.

I wasn't sure how hard to push back on this. Obviously, I couldn't insist that she legitimately looked really good, after she had been in the hospital for a week. No one looks good after that. Eventually, I went with, "You definitely look really good for someone who just had chemo," and she seemed to accept this.

"Thank you."

Then it was the end of visiting hours, and a nurse came in and told me I had to go, and if we're being honest, I sort of regretted that, just because I felt like I had done a mediocre job of cheering Rachel up and wanted to keep going for a bit. But if this makes me seem like a good person, it shouldn't. The reason was that cheering Rachel up was one of the things I had gotten really good at, and when you're good at something, you want to do it all the time, because it makes you feel good. So if I wanted to hang out with Rachel, it was mostly for selfish reasons.

"Wait, what's that drawing on your cast?" asked Mom, in the car.

"Oh, *those*," I said. My mind raced but I couldn't think of anything, so I had to just be honest. "Those are boobs."

"*Gross*," shrieked Gretchen, and we drove home, and then I ate normal food for the first time in a few days, and my stomach got all fucked up and trust me, you do not want to hear the details.

Chapter 24

PASTY TEEN HAS UNEVENTFUL DAY

It was about the second or third week of October when all this arm stuff happened. I think it was, anyway. I don't feel like looking it up. Do I have to give you a reason for not looking it up? I probably do, and that sucks. The reason that I probably should use is that it's just too emotionally painful, but obviously that's not true if I'm going to the trouble of writing this idiotic book. The real reason is: laziness. I thought about digging up the paperwork from my stay in the hospital and it just seemed like an unbelievable pain in the ass. So I didn't do it.

Also, it's weird to put a date to things anyway. It makes it feel like news or something. Like my life was in the *Post-Gazette* or the *New York Times*.

Oct. 20, 2011
PASTY TEEN RELEASED FROM HOSPITAL
Relieved Filmmaker Celebrates by Eating
Tummy Jiggling Leads to Cat Attack

Actually, yeah. This book is probably making my life seem more interesting and eventful than it actually is. Books always try to do that. If you just had headlines from every single day of my life you would get a better sense of how boring and random it is.

Oct. 21, 2011

PASTY TEEN MAKES QUIET RETURN TO SCHOOL

Gaines "Annoyed" by Backlog of Schoolwork

Numerous Teachers Failed to Notice Student's

Week-Long Absence

Oct. 22, 2011

NOTHING INTERESTING HAPPENS AT ALL

Even Dinner Was Leftovers

Oct. 23, 2011

FLABBY TEEN ATTEMPTS TO GROW MUSCLES ON

UNBROKEN ARM

Weight-Lifting Session Brief, Excruciating

Filmmaker Recovers with Hours Spent Motionless

Facedown on Floor of Room

Oct. 24, 2011

EXTREMELY LITTLE HAPPENS

Tummy Jiggling Leads to Cat Attack, Again

Student Has Series of Inane Conversations

Not Worth Going Into

Maybe after you die you get sent to a giant room with archives of newspapers that have been written by these angel journalists specifically about your life and then you read them and they look like this. That would be insanely depressing. Hopefully at least some of the headlines would be about the other people in your life and not just you.

Oct. 25, 2011

KUSHNER PURCHASES HAT

Awkward Staring at Bald Head Probably Became Annoying
After a While

Hat Somehow Even More Depressing Than
Darth Vader–Looking Head

Oct. 26, 2011

JACKSON UNLEASHES NICOTINE-DEPRIVED
LUNCHTIME TIRADE

Numerous People, Inanimate Objects, and
Concepts Said to Suck Donkey Dick

Plump Groundhog-Faced Friend:
Quitting Smoking "Probably a Mistake"

Oct. 27, 2011

GAINES PARENTS INITIATE NEW ROUND OF
COLLEGE TALKS

Filmmaker's "Disappointing" Grades Cited in
Detailed Predictions of Failure

Hobo Vocational College Considered

I guess when I was in the hospital, Mom and Dad decided that it was time to talk to me about colleges. It wasn't the first time we had discussed college, of course. The first time was when Dad walked into my room one day near the end of junior year. He had this sort of sheepish resentful look on his face that he gets when Mom asks him to do some really annoying thing.

"Hello, son," he had said.

"Hi," I said.

"Son, do you have any interest in going on a—a *college tour.*"

"Uh, not really."

"Oh!"

"Yeah, I don't really want to do that."

"No—*no* to the college tour, you're saying! I *see.*"

"Yeah, no."

Dad was so fired up about not doing a college tour that he immediately left the room and didn't mention it again for months. And even though college was kind of looming over my entire life during that time, as long as no one brought it up, I was able to ignore it.

For some reason I just really wasn't able to deal with the idea of college. I would try to think about it and then my mouth would get all dry and my armpits would start stinging and I would have to change the channel in my brain to something other than college. Usually it was to the Brain Nature Channel. That's where you picture a graceful herd of antelopes frolicking in the plains, or some playful beavers making a sophisticated little home out of twigs, or maybe one of those specials where they show Brazilian jungle insects biting the hell out of each other. Basically, anything until it no longer feels like your armpits have bees in them.

I don't know why college freaked me out so much. Actually, that's a blatant lie. I definitely know why. It had been a ridiculous amount of work figuring out life at Benson—mapping out the entire social landscape, figuring out all the ways to navigate it without being noticed—and it was pretty much at the limit of my espionage talents. And college is a much bigger, more complicated place than high school—like with infinitely more groups and people and activities—and so I got panicky and insane just thinking about how impossible it would be to deal with that. I mean, you're actually *living* with your classmates in a dormitory most of the time. How can you possibly be invisible to them? How can you just be sort of bland and inoffensive and unmemorable to the guys who are *living in your room*? You can't even fart in there. You have to go out into the hall or something to fart. Or you could just never fart, but then who knows what would happen.

So that was really terrifying to me and I didn't want to think about it. But then Mom and Dad decided that it was Important to Prepare For, and about a week after I got out of the hospital they ambushed me like a pair of Brazilian jungle insects and started biting the hell out of me. I mean, not literally. You know what I mean. It sucked.

After thinking about it a little bit, I figured I would just go to Carnegie Mellon, where Dad teaches. But Mom and Dad

were doubtful that I'd get in, because of my grades and total lack of extracurriculars.

"You could show them your films," suggested Mom.

This was such a terrible idea that I had to pretend to be dead for five minutes, which was how long it took Mom and Dad to get bored of yelling at me and leave the room. But then when they heard me moving around they came back and we had to talk some more.

In the end we decided that at the very least I should also apply to Pitt, a.k.a. the University of Pittsburgh, which I thought of at the time as Carnegie Mellon's larger, slightly dumber sibling. Mom also made me promise to just take a look at this directory of colleges, just maybe sit down for an hour and page through it, just to get some *ideas about what's out there*, it really won't take that long and it's just good to have some idea of your options because there are *so many different options out there* and it would *really be a shame if you didn't find the right one* and finally I was like OK OK JESUS CHRIST.

But the book of colleges was literally fourteen hundred pages long. So there was no way that was actually going to happen. For some reason I carried it around in my backpack for a few days and every time I looked at it I had the bees-in-the-armpits feeling.

I made the mistake of mentioning college around Rachel during one of my hospital visits, and then she got really interested in it and we had to talk about it for an awkwardly long time.

"Apparently, Hugh Jackman is doing this new ab workout,"

I said in an attempt to distract her. "So now he has four more abs than he used to have."

It's insane that that didn't distract her from college, but it didn't.

"So you want to go to Carnegie Mellon?" she said. She propped herself up and was sort of staring at me harder than usual.

"I mean, I'd rather go there than anywhere else," I said. "But Mom and Dad think I won't even get in. So I'll probably go to Pitt."

"Why wouldn't you get in?"

"Ugh, I don't know. You have to have good grades, and then additionally you have to be the president of a debate team, or you have to have built a homeless shelter, and I haven't done anything outside of school except fuck around."

I could tell Rachel wanted to bring up the films, but she didn't, which was good, because I was fully prepared to pretend to be dead again. But in a hospital that's less acceptable as a conversation-changing tactic. It's just not the right place to try that kind of move. Also, someone might walk in and actually think you're dead, and then they'd put you in a wheelchair and stick you out in a waiting room or something, like with Gilbert, the wheelchair-bound Possible Dead Person that I mentioned twenty-four hundred words ago.

"Really, my only goal with college is not to get into a fraternity," I said, just to get a decent riff going. "Because the number-one thing fraternities like to do is to take a fat kid and then tie him to a flagpole or a professor's car or something. So

I'm worried about that happening to me. That's their favorite thing to do. Maybe they would want to whip me with a belt or something. It's actually extremely homoerotic, but then if you point this out, they lose their shit."

For some reason this didn't make Rachel laugh.

"You're not fat," she said.

"I'm pretty fat."

"You're not."

It seemed stupid that Rachel was disagreeing with me. So the next thing I did was something I've never done before.

"I know of someone who disagrees with you," I said. "His name is Peanut Butter and Belly, minus the peanut butter."

"Huh," said Rachel, but then I lifted up my shirt and was showing her my belly.

I mean, I'm not as fat as a lot of kids, but I'm definitely fat, and I can definitely grab two different rolls of my stomach and make it talk like a Muppet.

"I WOULD LIKE TO TAKE ISSUE WITH WHAT YOU JUST SAID," yelled my stomach. It had a Southern accent for some reason. "I AM MORTIFIED AND DISTRESSED BY YOUR ACCUSATION. ADDITIONALLY, DO YOU HAVE ANY HEAPING PLATTERS OF NACHOS LYING ABOUT?"

Up until that point in my life I had never made my stomach talk for other human beings. It had just never seemed worth it to demean myself in that way for laughs. This should indicate how bad I wanted Rachel to laugh. But there was no snorting and honking from Rachel that day.

It's bad enough manhandling your own flabby stomach

and bellowing in a Southern accent at someone. It's worse when they're not even laughing at it.

"IF THERE ARE NO NACHOS, I WOULD BEGRUDG-INGLY SETTLE FOR A STEAK AND A CAKE," my stomach added, but Rachel did not even smile.

"What would you want to study at Carnegie Mellon?" she asked.

"Who knows?" I said. I was keeping my shirt up just in case she suddenly realized that I was making a total pathetic ass out of myself for her entertainment. But she didn't seem to be realizing it.

She was silent, so I kept talking. "I mean, most of the time you don't even know what you're gonna study when you show up to college anyway. So you just take a bunch of courses and you see what you like. Right?"

I had to keep riffing or she was going to ask about films. I could just tell. "It's like a buffet, basically. Like this really expensive buffet, except also you have to eat all of what's on your plate or they expel you. So conceptually that's kind of fucked up. If that happened at real buffets, that would be incredible. If you were like, 'Hmm, this moo shu pork has kind of a chalky dirt taste,' and then some enormous Chinese guy is like, 'EAT IT OR WE WILL GIVE YOU AN F, AND ALSO WE WILL KICK YOU OUT OF THIS RESTAURANT,' that just doesn't seem like a good business model."

Nothing. No snorting, no smiling. This really sucked. At this point I was holding up my shirt just to be stubborn, because it clearly was not going to produce any monster yuks.

"So you don't know what you want to study?"

Rachel was obviously driving at the film thing. But if she wasn't going to laugh at what I was saying, then fuck it. I decided to turn the whole thing on its head.

"No," I said. "I mean, what are *you* gonna study?"

Rachel just sort of stared at me.

"I mean, when you go to college, what are you gonna study?"

Rachel sort of turned her head away. I should have shut up at that moment but didn't.

"Where are you applying to college, anyway?"

Now Rachel was staring at the blank television screen and I was sitting there aiming my stupid fat stomach at her, and that was when it hit me that I was being a dick. Like, a colossal dick. I was asking a dying girl about her plans she's making for the future. That is just about the dickest move out there. Holy fuck. I wanted to punch myself in the face so bad. I wanted to slam a door on my head.

Although, at the same time, it's not like I stopped resenting her for being all sad and hostile and weird and making me feel bad for trying to cheer her up.

So basically I hated everyone in that room. I pulled my shirt down and tried to figure out a way to end this conversation without one of us trying to kill ourselves.

"Hey," I said. "Mom gave me this big-ass book of colleges. You can definitely have it if you want to look at some. I actually have it right now."

"I'm not applying to college this year."

"Oh."

"I'm gonna wait until I get better."

"That sounds like a good plan."

She continued to stare at the television screen, looking sort of blank and sort of pissed off.

"That's good," I said, "because this book sucks. It's like fourteen hundred pages long and every other page is about some random Christian place in Texas or something."

Can I tell you something? It was exhausting to keep coming up with these riffs. And maybe I should have just chilled out. But I felt like I had to make her laugh, or else my whole visit was a failure. So like some kind of brave seafaring adventurer, I embarked on another riff.

"Plus I get irritated because it's basically a reminder of how I'm not going to get into anywhere good. Like, you'll start from the end and then you get to 'Yale,' and you're like, Oh yeah, Yale, I should apply to there because it's a good school. All right. But then you see that they need at least a four point six grade point average. Yeah. And you're like, What the hell, Benson's grade point average doesn't even go *up* to four point six."

Rachel seemed to be softening up a little bit, although I felt like it was unrelated to the riff. But I decided to keep going with it because it was filling the time. Actually, that's the best thing about a good riff. It's not that it's funny, although usually a good riff is pretty funny. The most important thing is that it fills up the time so you don't have to talk about anything depressing.

"Yeah. And then you call their admissions office and you're like, Yale, what's up with this four point six business, and they're like, Oh, yeah, you know, if you were a more motivated student,

you would have discovered the *secret Yale preparation high school* that is buried deep beneath your normal high school, and all the teachers are these creepy *undead geniuses*, and that is the place where you would get a four point six or better, and also where you learn *the secrets of time travel.* And uh, and *creating artificial life out of ordinary household objects.* You can *bring the blender to li-i-i-i-ife.* The blender will become your devoted manservant *who gets you the mail*, except it accidentally *keeps tearing it into tiny pieces because it is a blender.* Ya-a-a-a-ale."

"Actually Greg, you can leave the book here."

There was a pretty good chance she was just saying this to get rid of me, but at least it was a response, and sort of a positive one.

"Seriously?"

"Unless you want to keep it."

"No. Are you kidding? I hate this book. This is great."

"Yeah, I want to look at it."

I fished it out of my backpack. I was really fired up to get rid of it. Also, maybe it was gonna make Rachel feel less like she was dying.

"Here you go."

"Just put it on the table."

"Done."

"OK."

She had maybe softened up a little bit, but she still wasn't laughing or responding very much at all and I sort of lost control a little and said, "I'm not cheering you up at all when I come here. I'm being a jackass."

"You're not being a jackass."

"I sort of am."

"Well, you don't have to come visit if you don't want."

This was kind of a tough thing to hear. Because, honestly, I *didn't* want to keep visiting her. It was stressful enough when she was in a *good* mood. Now that she was super-sick and pissed off all the time, it really stressed me out. It jacked up my heart rate, for example. I was sitting in there and I had that awful fluttery feeling you get in your heart when your heart rate is all jacked up. But I knew I would feel even worse if I didn't visit her.

So basically my life had been completely fucked up by all of this.

"I'm not coming here because I *don't want to*," I said. Then, because that didn't make any sense, I clarified: "I'm coming here because I want to. If I didn't want to come here, why the hell would I come here."

"Because you feel like you have to."

Really, the only thing I could do in response to this was lie.

"I don't feel like I *have to*. Also, I'm totally irrational and stupid. So sometimes when there are things I *have to do*, I don't even *do* them. I don't know how to live a *normal human life*."

This was a ridiculous direction to go in, so I backed up and started over.

"I *want* to come here," I said. "You're my friend."

Then I said, "I like you."

It felt ridiculously awkward saying that. I don't think I had ever said those words to anyone before, and I probably never will again, because you can't say them without feeling like a moron.

Anyway, she responded with: "Thanks." It was unclear how she meant it.

"Don't *thank* me."

"OK."

"I mean, sorry. This is insane. I'm yelling at you right now."

I wanted to get out of there. But I knew I'd feel like a dickbag just leaving. I guess she sensed this.

"Greg, I'm sick," she said. "I'm just not very cheerful right now."

"Yeah."

"You can go."

"OK, yeah."

"I like when you visit."

"That's good."

"Maybe I'll feel better next time."

But as it turned out, she didn't.

Jesus Christ I hate writing about this.

Chapter 25

A MORON'S GUIDE TO LEUKEMIA

So I should probably try to explain what leukemia is just in case you are confused about it. I knew extremely little about it before the whole Rachel thing. Now I know a mediocre amount, which frankly is much more than I am actually interested in knowing.

Some cancers are localized in your body, like lung cancer, or butt cancer. You probably think butt cancer doesn't exist, but it does. Anyway, with those cancers you can sometimes go in and cut them out surgically. But leukemia is cancer of the blood and bone marrow, so it's spread throughout your entire body, so you can't just go in and cut it out with knives. I mean, the knife thing obviously is scary and disgusting, but then the other way to treat cancer is to blast it with radiation and/or chemicals, which is worse. And with leukemia, you have to do that to someone's entire body.

So that definitely sucks.

Mom said it's like a city that has "bad guys" in it—something about the Rachel situation makes Mom forget that I'm not a toddler—anyway, it's like a city with bad guys and chemo is like

dropping bombs on the city to kill the bad guys. In the process, part of the city gets jacked up. I told Rachel about this, and she was dismissive.

"It's more like I have cancer," she said, "and I'm getting chemotherapy."

Anyway, in the process of bombing the bad guys to death, there was definitely some damage sustained by Rachel City, specifically in the neighborhoods of Hairville, Skinfield, and the Gastrointestinal District. That is why she bought the hat. It was this cute furry pink thing that you normally see on girls running around in shopping malls and not on pale girls lying in bed all the time.

So if this were a normal book about a girl with leukemia, I would probably talk a shitload about all the meaningful things Rachel had to say as she got sicker and sicker, and also probably we would fall in love and have some incredibly fulfilling romantic thing and she would die in my arms. But I don't feel like lying to you. She didn't have meaningful things to say, and we definitely didn't fall in love. She seemed less pissed with me after my stupid outburst, but she basically just went from irritable to quiet.

So I would go in there and say some things, and she would sort of smile and sometimes giggle a little bit but mostly just not say anything, and I would run out of things to say, and then we'd put on a Gaines/Jackson film and watch it. First the more recent ones, then the older ones when we got tired of those.

Watching them with her was a strange experience because

she was just so focused on them. I know it sounds idiotic, but sitting next to her, I suddenly saw the films the way I think she was seeing them—as this uncritical fan who actually *likes* all the stupid choices that we were making. I'm not saying I learned to enjoy watching the films. I guess I just saw how you might kind of tolerate all the insane imperfections and fuckups that we had. You might look at the bad lighting or the weird sound design and have your attention taken away from the story we were trying to tell and instead just be thinking about me and Earl, as filmmakers, sort of accidentally drawing attention to ourselves. And if you liked us, you would like that. That's maybe how Rachel was seeing everything we did.

But she didn't actually say anything, so maybe I was just making that all up.

And meanwhile, she didn't seem to be getting any better, and there were a couple of days where she was in a really dark mood and there was nothing I could do to help. Like one day when we were watching something and she had been really quiet and then she said, "Greg, I think you were right."

"What?"

"I said I think you were right."

"Oh."

She was quiet like she expected me to know what that meant.

"I'm, uh, usually right."

"Don't you want to know about what?"

"Uh, yeah."

Or maybe she didn't expect me to know what she meant.

Who knows? Girls are insane, and dying girls are even more insane. Actually, that sounds fucked up. I take that back.

"So I was right about what?"

"I think you were right when you said I was dying."

I hate complaining about this, but at the same time, this made me feel like shit. I was so pissed off that she said this. I tried to swallow it.

"I never said you were dying."

"You *thought* I was dying, though."

"No I didn't."

She was silent and it was infuriating.

"I *didn't*," I said, too loudly.

I mean, this was a lie, and we both knew it.

Finally, Rachel said, "Well, if you had thought it, you would have been right."

We were silent for a really long time after that. Actually, I wanted to yell at her. Maybe I should have.

JESUS CHRIST I HATE WRITING ABOUT THIS

Chapter 26

HUMAN FLESH

A person's life is like a big weird ecosystem, and if there's one thing science teachers enjoy blathering about, it's that changes in one part of an ecosystem affect the entire thing. So let's say my life is a pond. OK. Now let's say some insane person (Mom) shows up with this nonnative species of depressed fish (Rachel) and puts the fish in the pond. OK. The other organisms in the pond (films, homework) are used to having a certain amount of algae (time that I get to spend on those things) to eat. But now this cancer-stricken fish is eating all that algae. So the pond is sort of jacked up as a result.

(That last paragraph is so stupid that I couldn't even bring myself to delete it. By the way, for every mind-numbing thing that you have read in this book, there were like four other things that I wrote and then deleted. Most of them are about food or animals. I realize that I probably seem obsessed with food and animals. That's because they're the two strangest things in the entire world. Just sit in a room and think about them. Actually, don't, because you might have a panic attack.)

So that is what was happening in my life. My schoolwork was definitely suffering, for example. Mr. McCarthy even took me aside to talk about it.

"Greg."

"Hi, Mr. McCarthy."

"Purvey a fact for me."

Mr. McCarthy had ambushed me in the hall on the way to class. He was standing squarely in front of me and adopting an inexplicable stance. It was like the stance of a sumo wrestler, except with less stomping.

"Uh . . . any fact?"

"Any fact, but it must be presented with *extreme authority.*"

I wasn't getting a lot of sleep for some reason, so I actually had some trouble coming up with a fact.

"Fact: A change in one part of an ecosystem, uh, affects an entire thing."

Mr. McCarthy clearly wasn't impressed by this fact, but he let it go. "Greg, I'm gonna waylay you for five minutes. Then I'm gonna give you a note so you can go to class."

"Sounds good."

"That's what's about to happen, *right now.*"

"OK."

"Are you ready?"

"Yes."

"Good."

We walked into his office. They still hadn't finished rewiring the teachers' lounge, so the oracle was on his desk, presumably containing marijuana-infused soup. Seeing it, I immediately started panicking that Mr. McCarthy was going to confront me and Earl about drinking from the oracle. This panicky feeling got worse when Mr. McCarthy said the following thing:

"Greg, do you know why I brought you in here?"

There didn't seem to be a correct answer to that question. I'm pretty bad in pressure situations, also. This should not surprise you at all. So I tried to say "No," but my throat was dry from fear and I sort of just made a squeaking noise. I also probably looked like I was going to throw up. Because honestly, it was too stressful to think about what a big crazy tattoo-covered wacko like Mr. McCarthy would do if he knew we had discovered that he was doing something illegal. I was sitting there realizing that while I liked Mr. McCarthy, I was also deeply terrified of him and suspected that he might actually be a psychopath.

This suspicion deepened when, without warning, he tried to crush me with his giant brightly colored arms.

I was too terrified to fight back in any way, so I kind of just went limp. He had closed in on me and was sort of hugging me to death. A lot of thoughts were running through my head at that moment. One of them was: This is *exactly* the sort of dumb way a stoner would try to kill someone. By fatally hugging them. What is up with stoners? Drugs are asinine.

It took an embarrassingly long time to realize that he was actually just giving me a hug.

"Greg, bud," he said after a while. "I know how tough things are for you right now. With Rachel in the hospital. We've all seen it."

Then he let go. Because I had gone limp, this caused me to

fall most of the way down. Unlike your average high school student, Mr. McCarthy did not find this hilarious. Instead, he became very concerned.

"Greg!" he shouted. "Easy, bud. Do you need to go home?"

"No, no," I said. "I'm fine."

I got up. We sat down in chairs. Mr. McCarthy had a look on his face of deep concern. It was definitely out of character for him and it was sort of distracting me. It was like when a dog makes a human-style face at you and you're temporarily thrown off guard by it. You're like, "Whoa, this dog is feeling a mixture of nostalgic melancholy and proprietary warmth. I was not aware that a dog was capable of an emotion of that complexity."

That's what I was like with Mr. McCarthy.

"We've all seen how you've been affected by Rachel," said Mr. McCarthy. "And we've definitely heard about all this time you're spending with her. Bud, you're a great friend. Anyone would be lucky to have a friend like you."

"I'm really not," I said. Mr. McCarthy did not seem to hear me, which was probably good.

"And I know school is not your number one priority right now," added Mr. McCarthy, staring me in the eye in a way that was really nerve-racking. "I get that, bud. I was like you in school. I was smart, and I didn't apply myself, and I did just enough to get by. And until recently, *you've* been doing enough to get by. But hey."

He got closer to me. I was trying to imagine Mr. McCarthy

as a student. For some reason, in my head he was a ninja. He was sneaking around the cafeteria late at night, preparing to assassinate someone.

"Hey. Your schoolwork is definitely suffering. This is a true fact. I've talked to your other teachers. In all of your classes, you're unfocused, and you're not participating, and you're forgetting to do assignments. And in a few classes, bud, you're pretty deep underwater. Let me unload another fact on you. Rachel . . . doesn't want you . . . to fail your classes."

"Yeah," I said.

To be honest, I was pissed. Partially, I was pissed because Mr. McCarthy and I used to have this casual teacher-student relationship that involved zero earnest annoying talks like this, and that relationship was great. And now apparently it was over. And partially I was pissed because I knew he was right. I was definitely not doing all of my homework. Teachers had been pointing this out. I had been ignoring them, but it was harder to ignore Mr. McCarthy, because despite being an insane stoner, he was the only reasonable teacher in all of Benson.

"Bud, this is it," Mr. McCarthy said. "This is the last year, and then you're gone. Let me tell you this: After high school, life only gets better. You're in a tunnel right now. There's a light glimmering there at the end of it. You gotta make it to that light. High school is a *nightmare*, bud. It might be the worst years of your life."

I didn't really know what to say to this. The eye contact was giving me a headache.

"So you gotta make it out. You can't fail. You've got the best excuse in the world right now, but you can't use it. All right?"

"Yeah."

"I'm gonna do everything I can for you, because you're a good kid. Greg, you're a fucking great kid."

I had never heard Mr. McCarthy use the F-word, so this at least was sort of exciting. Still, my Excessive Modesty reflex would not be denied.

"I'm not that great of a kid."

"You're an absolute beast," said Mr. McCarthy. "That's all there is to it. Get to class. Here's a note. We all think you're a *total . . . ferocious . . . beast.*"

The note said: "I had to meet with Greg Gaines for five minutes. Please excuse his absence. He is a beast. –Mr. McCarthy, 11:12 am."

Meanwhile, at home, Gretchen was going through this phase where she could not make it through an entire meal if Dad was at the table. This was in part because Dad was going through a phase of his own wherein he couldn't stop pretending to be a cannibal. If we were eating anything with chicken in it, he would pat his stomach and announce, "Huma-a-a-an flesh. TASTE LIKE CHICKEN." This caused Gretchen to burst into tears and stomp out of the dining room. Things only got worse when Grace started doing it, too, which was insane, because a six-year-old pretending to be a cannibal is one of the greatest things there is.

So that's what was going on at home. Actually, that's not even relevant, but I wanted to write about the cannibal thing.

And as for filmmaking, I dunno. Earl and I didn't really end up doing the *Two Poncy Dudes* movie. We met up a few times to watch David Lynch films, and we knew that he kicked ass, but for some reason we were having trouble coming up with a script of our own. We'd kind of just sit around staring at the laptop screen. Then Earl would go outside for a cigarette and I would follow him. Then we'd come back and do more wordless staring.

So you're probably reading all this, and being like, "Wow, Greg was really sad about Rachel, to the point where his entire life was in this tailspin. That is sort of touching." But honestly, that's not accurate. It's not like I was sitting in a room, with tears running down my face, clutching one of Rachel's bedroom pillows and listening to harp music all the time. I wasn't wandering any dewy meadows, ruefully meditating on the Happiness We Could Have Had. Because maybe you don't remember this, but I really didn't love Rachel at all. If she hadn't had cancer, would I be spending any time with her at all? Of course not. In fact, if she were to make a miraculous recovery, would we stay friends after that? I'm not even sure if we would. This all obviously sounds terrible, but there's no point in lying about it.

So I wasn't sad. I was just exhausted. When I wasn't at the hospital, I felt guilty for not being at the hospital trying to cheer Rachel up. When I was at the hospital, most of the time I felt ineffective and useless as a friend. So either way, my life was deeply fucked up. But I also felt like a moron feeling sorry for

myself, because I was not the one whose life was literally about
to end.

At least I had Earl some of the time to cheer me up.

EXT. GAINES BACK PORCH — EVENING

                    EARL
                suddenly
        So you can be a heterosexual, or
        a homosexual, and I feel like I
        understand that, like you're a woman in
        a man's body or some shit, but I been
        thinking about it and how the fuck can
        somebody call theyself a *bi*sexual.

                    GREG
        Uhh . . .

                    EARL
        Man, ain't nobody like, that fine-ass
        girl is making me hard right now. Oh
        wait, my mistake, that *dude* over there
        is the one that's making me hard. That
        don't make no goddamn *sense*.

                    GREG
        I guess sometimes I also wonder about
        that.

EARL

Goddamn. If you're seriously like,
"For real, I'm a bisexual, any person
can get me hard," man, you must get
a hard-on from all kinds of freaky
shit.

GREG

I think, uh . . . I mean, some
scientists think that everyone's
actually a little bit of both. Homo
and hetero.

EARL

Naw. That don't make any damn sense
at all. You tellin me right now, you
can look at some titties, get a hard-
on, look at some dude's funky dick,
get another hard-on. You gonna tell
me that for real.

GREG

I guess I can't say that, no.

EARL

determinedly

Dog taking a dump: hard-on. Wendy's
double cheeseburger: hard-on.

Computer virus that destroy all your
shit: hard-on.

                    GREG
Business section of the *Wall Street
Journal.*

                    EARL
Big-ass hard-on for *that shit.*

Contemplative silence.

                    EARL
Yo, I got a line for you. You wanna
get with that girl, with the big-ass
titties?

                    GREG
Yeah, give me a line.

                    EARL
You walk up to her, say, Girl, you
might not a known this about me, but
I'm a *trisexual.*

                    GREG
          uncertainly
OK.

                    EARL
Girl's like, What the fuck?

                    GREG
Yeah.

                    EARL
You like, Yeah, *tri*sexual.

                    GREG
OK.

                    EARL
She like, Whaaaaaat. You with me?

                    GREG
I'm with you.

                    EARL
Awright, she all confused. Then
you drop the bomb, you're like:
trisexual, girl. Cuz I'ma *try* to
have *sex* with you.

                    GREG
Ohhhhhh!

                    EARL
Try-sexual.

                    GREG
I'll definitely use that.

                    EARL
Mack.

Chapter 27

YOU AND ME AND A PERPETUALLY EXPLODING TURKEY MAKES THREE

All right. Now we're reaching the part where my life really started accelerating toward the edge of a cliff. And actually, this part wasn't even Mom's fault! It was Madison's. It's definitely messed up that they played similar roles in my life. I'm trying not to think about this too hard, lest I never get a boner ever again.

It was the beginning of November, and I was in the part of the hall where they had tacked up a bunch of vaguely terrifying pilgrim-and-turkey paintings by the ninth graders, when Madison appeared out of nowhere and grabbed my arm. Our skin was actually touching, specifically in the hand-to-arm format.

Suddenly, I became terrified that I was going to belch.

"Greg," she said. "I have a favor to ask you."

It wasn't like I felt a belch forming in my stomach. It was just that, in my mind's eye, I could foresee myself belching at Madison. I saw this extremely vividly. Maybe there would be a small amount of barf in there.

"So I promise I haven't seen any of your movies," she said,

sort of a little impatiently, "but Rachel has, obviously, and she really likes them. And I just had this idea—you should make a movie for *her*."

I wasn't really sure what this meant. Also, to distract myself from the Belch of Doom that was lurking in my esophagus, I was looking away at a picture of a turkey. It was not all that well drawn. For some reason it seemed to have blood shooting out of all parts of its body. It was probably supposed to be feathers, or rays of the sun, or something.

"Huh," I said.

Meanwhile, Madison sounded confused by my unenthusiastic reaction to her idea.

"I mean," she said, and stopped. "Don't you think she would love that?"

"Hummmm."

"Greg, what are you looking at?"

"Uh, sorry, I got distracted."

"By what?"

I really couldn't think of anything. It was like I was on drugs. In fact, that reminded me of the inexplicable badger picture that showed up in my head after Earl and I ate Mr. McCarthy's pho. So I said, "Uh, there was just this badger picture in my head for some reason."

It goes without saying that the moment those words left my lips, I wanted to do serious injury to myself.

"Badger," Madison repeated. "Like the animal?"

"Yeah, you know," I said feebly. Then I added: "Just one of those badger head pictures you sometimes get."

I wanted to eat a power tool. Incredibly, however, Madison was able to ignore this and move on.

"So I think you should make a movie for Rachel. She just really loves your movies so much. She watches them all the time. They make her so happy."

As if the badger thing weren't enough, it had suddenly become time for me to say a second stupid thing. Actually, it was time for another episode of everyone's least favorite show, *Excessive Modesty Hour with Greg Gaines.*

"They can't make her *that* happy."

"Greg, shut up. I know you have issues with being complimented. Just take a compliment for once, because it's *true.*"

Madison had actually observed and remembered one of my personality traits. This was so astonishing that I said, "Word," completing a personal trifecta of Consecutive Inane Utterances That Will Prevent Sex from Ever Happening.

"Did you just say 'Word'?"

"Yeah, word."

"Huh."

"Word, like, I agree."

Madison, crafty girl that she is, managed to turn this last one on its head.

"So you agree! To make a movie! For Rachel!"

What the hell could I possibly say to that? Except yes?

"Uh, yeah. Yeah! I think it's a good idea."

"Greg," she said, with a huge lovely smile, "this is going to be *amazing.*"

"Maybe it'll be good!"

"I know you are going to make something *wonderful*."

So I felt deeply conflicted here. On the one hand, basically the hottest nice girl in the entire school was telling me how great I was and how great of a film I was going to make. So that felt really good and was making me stand funny to hide a partial boner. On the other hand, though, I was agreeing to a project that I had grave doubts about. Actually, I didn't even know what I was agreeing to.

So I said, "Uh."

Madison waited for me to continue. The problem was I wasn't even sure what to say.

"One thing, though," I said.

"Mmmmm?"

"What, uh. Uhhhmmmmm."

"What?"

"It's just, uh."

There seemed to be no way of asking this question without sounding like a moron.

"What do you think," I said carefully, "the film should *be*."

Madison now had kind of a blank look.

"You should just make a movie," she said, "that's specifically for her."

"Yeah, but, uh."

"Just make the movie that you would want to get if you were Rachel."

"But what should it be, uh, *about?* D'you think."

"I dunno!" said Madison cheerfully.

"OK."

"Greg, you're the director. It's your movie!"

"I'm the director," I said. I was really starting to lose focus. I felt the distant rumblings of a major freak-out coming on.

"I have to run. I'm so happy you're doing this!" she exclaimed.

"Yeahhhh," I said weakly.

"You're the best," she said, hugging me. Then she ran away.

"Burp," I said, when she was out of earshot.

The exploding turkey had an expression on his face, like: "Goddammit! I'm exploding *again?*"

Chapter 28

RACHEL THE FILM: BRAINSTORMING

Earl had even less of an idea of how to do this project than I did. However, he was much better at articulating that.

"The *fuck*," he kept muttering as I was trying to describe the project to him.

"Look," he finally said. "You agreed to make a film *for* somebody. Now what the hell do *that* mean."

"Uh, I guess . . . It means . . . Huh."

"Yeah. You got no idea what the hell it mean."

"I feel like I sort of do."

"Well, spit it out, son."

We were in my kitchen and he was rummaging through our food, which put him in at least a neutral mood, if not a good one.

"I mean, if we were painters, we could just paint a picture of something and give it to her as a gift. Right? So let's just do the film version of that."

"Where the hell do Pa Gaines keep the salsa at."

"I think we're out. Look—what if we just did a one-off film? And gave her the only copy? That works, right?"

"Son, that don't give oh, *hot damn.*"

"What?"

"What the hell is *this.*"

"That's—lemme look at it."

"This smell like a donkey's hairy-ass *dick.*"

"Ohhhh. This is goose-liver pâté."

"There ain't no salsa, I'ma eat *this* shit."

As I've mentioned before, Earl gets very fired up about the occasionally gross animal-derived foods purchased and refrigerated by Dr. Victor Q. Gaines. I say "purchased and refrigerated" because Dad never eats them right away. He likes for them to spend a lot of time in the fridge, so that the rest of the family has a chance to become aware of them. It's a habit that Gretchen may hate more than anything else in the world. However, Gretchen's extreme dislike is balanced by the almost-as-extreme appreciation of Earl. Earl expresses his appreciation by talking about how disgusting the food is while eating it.

"Son. We still have no idea what the film gonna be about."

"Yeah, that's the hard part."

"Yeah."

"Uhhhh."

"Like, we could make the David Lynch film that we was

gonna make, and just give it to Rachel, and that's her film. But I don't think we want to do that."

"No?"

"Hell no. That'd be weird as hell. We'd be like, Yo, Rachel, watch this crazy-ass film about lesbians running around and hallucinating and shit. We made this film especially for you."

"Huh."

"Like at the beginning, it's like, 'For Rachel.' It's like we're saying: Rachel, *you* love David Lynch. *You* love freaky-ass lesbians getting they freak on. So here's a film about that shit. Nah. That don't make no sense. Now what the fuck is *this*."

"No, no, don't eat that. That's dried cuttlefish. That's like Dad's favorite. He likes to wander around with part of it sticking out of his mouth."

"I'ma take a little bite."

"You can like nibble it once, but that's it."

"Mmm."

"What do you think?"

"Man, this taste stupid. This taste like some kinda . . . undersea . . . urinal."

"Huh."

"It taste like dolphins and shit."

"So, you don't like it."

"I did *not* say that."

"Oh."

"Yeah, it's like seventy-five percent dolphin scrotum, twenty-five percent chemicals."

"So you *do* like it."

"This is a dumb-ass piece of food."

I had to agree with Earl: We couldn't just do any film. There had to be at least some kind of connection to Rachel's life. But what connection could that be? We sat in the kitchen and we brainstormed a bunch of them. All of the ideas were stupid.

They were really stupid. You're about to see exactly how stupid. I mean, my God.

"Are you done eating that?"

"What?"

"You shouldn't finish that, Dad's gonna want some."

"The hell he will."

"He will."

"It's so nasty. Son, it's *so* nasty."

"Then why are you finishing it?"

"Takin a bullet."

Chapter 29

RACHEL THE FILM: THE HALLMARK VERSION

I knew our first plan was a mistake when Jared "Crackhead" Krakievich waddled up to me in the hall and addressed me as "Spielberg."

"Hah yih doin, Spillberg," he shouted, grinning hideously.

"What?" I said.

"I seen yer maykin' a *mewvie*."

"Oh yeah."

"I dinn *know* yih made mewvies."

"Just this one," I said, probably too hastily.

"I'm call yih Spillberg fruh now on."

"Great."

It was the first shot fired in a nightmarish barrage of attention that would continue all day.

Mrs. Green, Physics 1 I.S.: "I think what you are doing is so . . . *touching* and . . . *remarkable,* and just really touching."

Kiya Arnold: "My cousin *died* of leukemia. I just want to say.

I'm so sorry about your girlfriend. How long y'all been together?"
Will Carruthers: "Hey faggot! Lemme be in your gay movie."

Plan A was: Get the well-wishes of everyone at school,
synagogue, etc., and put them in a film, and have that be the film.
A get-well film, basically. Simple, elegant, heartwarming. Sounds
like a good idea, right? Of course it does. We were completely
seduced by this idea. We were morons.

**First Problem: We had to get the footage ourselves, meaning
we had to reveal ourselves as filmmakers to a hostile world.**
Originally, I asked Madison if she would get the footage herself,
i.e., if *she* would hang out in a classroom with a camera instead
of me and Earl. This led to me saying that I sort of didn't want
people knowing I was making a film for Rachel, which made her
upset. *That* led to me saying that I didn't want people to know
about my *feelings* for Rachel, which made her upset in a different
way that I did not, frankly, understand. Anyway, she insisted that
I get the footage, and said "Oh, Greg" about seventy times until
I quietly freaked out and ran away.

So we made plans to film in Mr. McCarthy's room after
school, and reluctantly told a couple of teachers about it, and
with disturbing speed all teachers had found out about it, and
told their students, and also it made the morning announcements
every day in a row for like a week.

So yeah. This was possibly the death blow to the invisibility I
had been cultivating throughout high school, and then gradually

losing since becoming friends with Rachel. I used to be just normal Greg Gaines. Then I was Greg Gaines, Rachel's Friend and Possibly Boyfriend.

That was bad enough. But now I was Greg Gaines, Filmmaker. Greg Gaines, Guy with a Camera, Following People Around. Greg Gaines, Perhaps He Is Creepily Filming You Right Now Without Your Knowledge or Consent.

Fuckbiscuit.

Second Problem: The footage was not very good. The teachers all ran way too long, first of all. None of them said anything that could be edited down. A lot of them started talking about tragedies that had happened in *their* lives, which besides being unusable made things fairly awkward in the room after they were done recording.

As for the students, 92 percent said some combination of these things:

- "Get better."
- "I have to say I don't know you that well."
- "I know we never hung out very much."
- "You're in my class, but we've never really talked."
- "I actually don't know anything about you."
- "But I do know that you have the inner strength to get better."
- "You have a beautiful smile."
- "You have a beautiful laugh."
- "You have really beautiful eyes."

- "I think your hair is beautiful."
- "I know you're Jewish, but I'd like to just say something from the Bible."

And then the other 8 percent tried to be funny or creative, and that was even worse.

- "In eighth period, I wrote a song that I want to sing you. Are we ready? Can I just sing it? OK. Rachel Kushner / Don't you push her / She's got leukemia / and she probably wants to scream-ia / But she's everybody's friend! / You know her life's not gonna end!!!"
- "Even if you do die, I was thinking today, it's really only on the arbitrary human scale that a human life seems short, or long, or whatever, and, like, from the perspective of eternal time, the human life is vanishingly small, like it's really equivalent whether you live to be 17 or 94 or even 20,000 years old, which is obviously impossible, and then, on the other hand, from the perspective of an ultra-nanoinstant, which is the smallest measurable unit of time, a human life is almost infinite even if you die when you're, like, a toddler. So either way it doesn't even matter how long you live. So I don't know if that makes you feel better, but it's just something to think about."
- "Greg's a fag. I guess he's in love with you, so that makes him bisexual or whatever. I hope you feel better."

Third Problem: Madison had already made get-well cards for Rachel. So we weren't really doing anything new, for one. We were just doing a get-well card in video form.

Also—this took a little longer to realize—there was nothing specifically Gaines/Jackson about the get-well video. It was something anyone could do. So was it really that great of a gesture? No.

We'd been making films for seven years. We needed to do something better.

Chapter 30

RACHEL THE FILM: THE KEN BURNS VERSION

Ken Burns has done a bunch of documentaries about things, like the Civil War. He wasn't around for the Civil War, just like we weren't really around for most of Rachel's life. I mean, we were, but we weren't paying attention. That sounds horrible, but you know what I mean. Or, maybe it's just horrible. I don't know.

Look: We haven't been following Rachel around with a camera for her entire life in order to get footage for an eventual documentary. You can't really get mad at me for that.

Anyway, the Ken Burns style is to show a bunch of photos and old footage taken by other people, along with voiceovers and interviews and stuff. It's a very easy style to copy, so this was our designated Plan B after the get-well video idea failed. Unfortunately, we really only had one person to interview: Denise. And Denise was going through a rough time. Her only child had cancer, and Rachel's father—I probably forgot to mention this earlier—was estranged from the family.

Interviewing this woman was a total nightmare.

INT. KUSHNER LIVING ROOM — DAY

          GREG
      offscreen
So, Denise. Can you tell me a bit
about Rachel's birth?

          DENISE
      distractedly
Oh, Rachel's birth.

          GREG
      offscreen
Yes.

          DENISE
Rachel's birth. What an ordeal.
     inexplicably loudly
She was never much of a fighter.
She's always been a quiet girl, just
so sweet, never wanting to fight,
and now I don't know what to do. I
can't make her fight, Greg.

          GREG
      offscreen
Uh, right.

                    DENISE
I raised a girl who's sweet, and . . .
and lovely, but not tough.

                    GREG
          offscreen
So what was she like as a baby? Did
she have a favorite toy?

                    DENISE
          distractedly
She used to read . . . books.
          uncomfortable pause
Greg, I'm a good mother. But I don't
know how to get her through this.
It's like, God forbid, she doesn't
want to live anymore.

                    GREG
          offscreen
So, as a baby, she liked to . . .
read books.

                    DENISE
          firmly, sort of robotically
I'm a good mother. I've been a good
mother to her.

We made an attempt to interview Rachel's grandparents over the phone, but that was possibly an even more depressing failure.

"Hello?"

"Hi, Mr. Lubov—this is Greg, a friend of Rachel's."

"Who?"

"A friend of your granddaughter, Rachel."

"*Whose* friend?"

"Your granddaughter. Rachel."

"Hang on. (Janice. It's for you. *I said it's for you.* The *phone*. No, I don't know where it is. The *phone*, Janice.)"

" . . . "

"Who is this?"

"Hi, my name is Greg. I'm a friend of your granddaughter, Rachel."

"Rachel lives . . . Rachel lives with her mother."

"I know—I'm doing a documentary? About Rachel?"

"You're doing a—oh."

"I was wondering if I could ask you some questions?"

"What?"

"Can I ask you some questions about Rachel?"

"Ask her mother. Denise."

"It's for a film, to make her happy."

"OK, I don't know who you are, and I don't know how to help you. But if you're looking for Rachel, she lives with her mother, Denise."

"Um . . . OK, thanks."

I hung up because it sounded like Rachel's grandma was

about to cry. But sometimes grandmas just sound like that. Either way: excruciating.

There wasn't much footage lying around for us to use, either. There was one vacation video that Denise let us look at, but we were really hesitant to use it.

EXT. BEACH, PRINCE EDWARD ISLAND — DAY

The sky is gray. The sand is dark, as though it has just rained. It looks as though it may rain again. RACHEL is sitting heavily on a towel, doing nothing, facing the sea.

                    DENISE
               offscreen
          Hi honey!

Rachel turns to face the camera and says nothing. Her face is expressionless.

                    DENISE
               offscreen
          Here we are on beautiful Prince
          Edward Island. There's little Rachel,
          and there's Bill.

PAN to BILL, next to an umbrella. He is in an elaborate beach chair with TWO BEER HOLDERS, both containing beers.

> BILL
> *too loudly*
> We're having a GREAT TIME.

> DENISE
> *offscreen, fake cheerful*
> Bill's a little grumpy because of the weather!

> BILL
> Denise, can you just turn that thing off.

> DENISE
> *offscreen*
> Can you at least try to enjoy yourself.

> BILL
> What does it LOOK LIKE I'M DOING.

Let's put it this way: If I were Rachel, lying in bed feeling awful, this would not make the list of Scenes I Would Want to Be Watching in a Movie.

And actually, *everything* we put together via the Ken Burns method failed that test. In essence, we were trying to put together a biography of a girl who hadn't lived very long and hadn't really had that interesting of a life. I know that sounds horrible, but it's true. None of it was interesting to watch. And a lot of it was sort of painful.

And then taken as a whole, the documentary-of-Rachel's-life idea was *really* painful, because we never came out and said it, but basically the message was: Now that your life is over, we can summarize it. So here's a summary of all of your life. There maybe isn't a worse thing that we could have said.

So we needed a new method. And it needed to be much better. Otherwise, we were going to kill ourselves.

Meanwhile, things were going shitty with Rachel. I mean, it was usually just more of the same.

INT. HOSPITAL ROOM — EVENING

                    GREG
        So I was thinking today: Strawberry
        is my favorite flavor of candy. But I
        don't actually like strawberries that
        much. And then I realized, strawberry-
        flavored candy doesn't actually taste
        like strawberries at all. So what does
        it taste like? That's got to be the
        taste of *something*, right? Is there
        this delicious mystery fruit out there

that I don't know about? I want to eat
that fruit, you know? I want to eat
the hell out of it.

Or then I was thinking, does an *animal*
maybe taste like that? Like maybe if
you ate, I don't know, a walrus, it
would have that awesome taste, but the
guys who make Airheads are afraid to
say, walrus-flavored Airheads.

RACHEL
weakly

Yeah.

GREG

Yo, is that a new pillow? I think
that's a lady pillow over there.
Hey . . .

whispering

Would you mind introducing me to her?
Because she's totally fine. You don't
have to if it's awkward.

RACHEL
possibly trying to laugh

hhhhnnh

                    GREG
              panicking
Holy shit, I forgot. What time is
it? It's after five? I have to do
Pigeon Man. Sorry, it's part of my
new exercise regimen.
              crossing eyes, bobbing head,
              strutting
PIGEON MAN. PIGEON MAN. WALKS LIKE A
PIGEON. PIGEON MAN. POOPS ON YOU, *FROM*
THE SKY. HE'S THE PIGEON-EST MAN.

                    RACHEL
Greg, you don't have to — try to
make me laugh.

                    GREG
What?

                    RACHEL
You don't have to put on — a show.

                    GREG
              feeling like shit
OK.

Chapter 31

RACHEL THE FILM: THE SOCK PUPPET VERSION

Plan C was sock puppets.

First of all, let me just say that sock puppets can be way more emotional and expressive than they get credit for. There are a lot of different ways to put your hand in a sock and make it look like a face. Also, if you draw eyebrows over the eyes, that's really humanizing. You have to know what you're doing with the mouth, but if you do, you can make magic happen.

All that said, Plan C was a cancer-themed movie starring sock puppets. So it was pretty much doomed from the get-go.

Once we decided to try sock puppets, our main problem was plot. If Rachel was the star, what did she do? Whose ass did she kick? Was she going to kick leukemia's ass?

```
INT. BRIGHTLY COLORED CARDBOARD LANDSCAPE
— DAY


            RACHEL
     La di da di da
```

                    LUKE
          wearing cape and mustache,
          speaking with a Southern accent
Howdy!

                    RACHEL
          suspiciously
Hmmm. Who are you.

                    LUKE
Uh . . . my name is Luke.

                    RACHEL
What's your *full* name.

                    LUKE
Luke mmmphlmmph.

                    RACHEL
I can't *hear you.*

                    LUKE
Luke Emia.

                    RACHEL
TIME FOR A BEATDOWN.

How did this make us better than Justin Howell? The theater kid who wrote the song about how leukemia made Rachel want to scream-ia? We weren't sure.

INT. BRIGHTLY COLORED CARDBOARD LANDSCAPE — DAY

           LUKE EMIA
         addressing camera
What's up, this is a public service announcement. I'm leukemia. I like to pick on kids and teenagers, because I'm extremely pathetic. Here's a list of things I hate:

— delicious foods such as pizza
— adorable panda cubs
— if you were to fill an Olympic-size swimming pool with pleasant-smelling rubber balls such as would be fun to frolic around in, I would hate that as well.

Not a lot of people know this, but my favorite thing in the world is a poorly made car commercial with generic guitar music in the backGROUN GAARRGGHH

RACHEL, holding a baseball bat in her mouth, clubs LUKE while yodeling.

It was just all really childish and simplistic. It had nothing to do with anything. It looked like television for toddlers, and even worse, it was a big stupid lie. Rachel wasn't fighting leukemia. She wasn't interested in fighting. She seemed like she was giving up.

Chapter 32

RACHEL THE FILM: THE WALLACE & GROMIT VERSION

Plan D was stop-motion animation. In stop-motion animation, you shoot a single frame of something, move the characters slightly and maybe also the camera, shoot another frame, move things again, etc. It's painstaking and time-consuming. On the plus side, it allows you to use LEGO Darth Vader.

We wanted Rachel to watch a bunch of evil people talking about how much they love leukemia, and get pissed off at them, and be inspired to fight back. This led to some terrible filmmaking.

```
INT. LEGO DEATH STAR — NIGHT, WHICH IT
ALWAYS IS IN SPACE

Elevator music. LEGO stormtroopers are
wandering around in the background.
```

DARTH VADER

singing to himself

La la la. I am a jackass. Doot di
doo. Big, big jerk.

looking at camera

Oh! Hello! I didn't see you there.
My name is Darth Vader, and I'm the
president of Evil Villains In favor
of Leukemia, a.k.a. EVIL.

Appearing in the lower left-hand corner:
Evil
Villains
In favor of
Leukemia

DARTH VADER

We just think leukemia is the
greatest. But don't take my word for
it! Here's some testimony from some
annoying pirates!

EXT. LEGO PIRATE SHIP — DAY

PIRATE KING

Arrrr! 'Twas a day the likes o'

no other, athwart the starboard bow
upon the rottin' maggoty beard o'
Davy Jones hisself!!! Upon the
horizon did Two-Eyepatch Bill not
espy the hideous sucker'd limbs o'
the mighty Kraken — fast amidships
all cannons astern and swab the
decks,ye filthy motherless bilge rat
SWINE!!!!!

INT. DEATH STAR — NIGHT

> DARTH VADER
>
> Uh . . . sure.

INT. GREG'S DESK — DAY

> PLASTIC FIGURINE OF
> SERPENTOR
> *with a snake accent*
> I am Serpentor, Cobra Emperor, of
> the evil Cobra Command! Leukemia is
> my favorite thing in the *world*! Now,
> because I love leukemia so much, I am
> going to go make out with my *sister*,
> the Baroness Anastasia DeCobray! You

can tell she's evil because her last
name has the word "Cobra" in it!

> BARONESS
>
> I love making out with my nasty-ass
> brother! Because I'm disgusting as
> hell!!

> SERPENTOR
>
> How do we kiss again?

> BARONESS
>
> My goddamn mouth won't open.

> SERPENTOR
>
> Neither will mine.

> BARONESS
>
> The hell we supposed a do now.

INT. DEATH STAR — NIGHT

> DARTH VADER
>
> We sure do love leukemia! Don't
> believe me yet? Why don't you ask this
> spinning tarantula paperweight?

INT. GREG'S DESK — DAY

The tarantula paperweight is a dead
tarantula encased in glass. The magic of
stop-motion animation is causing it to spin
around in a circle.

      SPINNING TARANTULA
      PAPERWEIGHT
      with a German accent for some
      reason
    Nothing makes me happier than
    leukemia.

Christ.

So this was Plan D. Maybe it would have been good. I don't know. I doubt it. What I do know is, it took forever to do, and a few days before Thanksgiving break, Rachel and Denise decided that they were done with chemotherapy, and being in the hospital, and getting treatment. They were just going to let things run their course, they decided.

At that point I didn't really know what to do.

Chapter 33

JESUS, NOW WHAT AM I SUPPOSED TO DO

So Rachel moved back to her room. Things were different, obviously. Actually, she was in a pretty good mood those first few days. The first day she came back was a Friday. It was late November but not cold yet.

"They've stopped shooting me up with chemicals," she explained.

"So that's over?"

"They just didn't seem to be doing me any good."

We silently contemplated this morbid utterance. For some reason, I said, "Certainly not in the hair department." I was trying to make things less depressing, which of course had the effect of making things *more* depressing. But Rachel actually laughed. It was sort of a different kind of laugh, like she had to reengineer the shape of her mouth during laughter, because the old way was too painful. I did a surprisingly good job of not thinking about this.

Pretty soon I was just talking a lot and I wasn't trying too hard to make her laugh and it felt a lot like before she went to the

hospital and got all depressed. We were just sprawled out in her kind of dark poster-and-pillow-intensive room and I was going on at insane length about my life and she was just listening and absorbing it all and it felt like we were back on normal terms with each other. It was possible to forget that she had decided to die.

By the way, when someone stops cancer treatment and you point out that this is a decision to die, everyone freaks out at you. Mom, for example. I don't even want to get into it.

But yeah.

"So Gretchen is just acting nuts."

"Oh yeah?"

"Oh man. Girls at that age are just impossible. There's just a lot of shrieking and stomping around. Some of it doesn't even make any sense. Were you like that? At like age fourteen?"

"I fought with my mom sometimes."

"Gretchen even gets pissed off at *Cat Stevens*. She'll be petting him and then he'll freak out and bite her, which he's been doing for his entire life, and then suddenly she's like, Oh my God, I fucking *hate stupid Cat Stevens*. She says he looks like a big garden slug. Which he does, obviously, but that's sort of what's so great about him."

"That he looks like a slug?"

"Yeah, he's just this ugly stripey slug color. He's like the biting champion of the slug world."

I guess it actually wasn't possible to *completely* forget that she had decided to die. Because the whole time as we were talking, it was in the back of my mind and it was stressing me out a little bit, the idea that Rachel was close to the end of her life. Or not stressing me out, but just kind of weighing on me and making me feel a little short of breath.

Eventually, Rachel said, "How's your latest film coming?"

"Oh, the latest one! Yeah. It's pretty good."

"I'm really excited to see it."

Something about the way she said this made me realize that she knew about it. I mean, it was stupid to think she wouldn't find out.

"Yeah, uh . . . Hey. You should probably know: It's for you. Like, it's sort of about you, and uh, yeah."

"I know."

I was trying to be cool about this.

"Oh, you knew that already?"

"Yeah, some people told me."

"Uh, like who?" I was talking kind of loud and high-pitched. I actually sounded a little like Denise Kushner at that moment.

"I don't know. Madison told me about it. Mom sort of mentioned it. Anna, Naomi. Earl. A few people."

"Oh," I said. "Uh. That reminds me. I have to go talk to Earl about something."

"OK," she said.

Chapter 34

FIGHT CLUB, EXCEPT LAMER

Earl and I had never been in a fight. That was mostly because I am cowardly, and also partially because we had a pretty good working relationship with well-defined roles. The point is, I had never really gotten angry at him, and also I am terrified of conflict. Especially with Earl, because of the windmill kick to the head that he can do.

But I was pissed that he had told Rachel. So I went over to his house to yell at him.

Even just writing about this is giving me sharp stabbing armpit pains.

The whole time on the walk over I was kind of muttering to myself. Specifically, I was rehearsing the stuff that I was going to say.

"Earl," I muttered to myself, "the foundation of any good working relationship is trust. And I can no longer trust you in any way. By telling Rachel about this film, which was supposed to be a surprise, you have betrayed my trust."

I was lurching through the streets of Earl's not-so-great part of Homewood, moving my lips, making semi-coherent noises, walking faster than is graceful for an overweight person to walk, and emitting maybe a quart of human sweat.

"I don't know if I can work with you again. You will have to earn my trust back if you want to work with me. I don't even know how you would go about doing that."

I was on his block, and the sight of his ramshackle weird house jacked up my heart rate even worse than it had already been jacked up.

"You're going to need to convince me that I can trust you." That was another inane thing that I said.

I walked up the walk where I had broken my arm, and stood there, no longer muttering. Somehow I was terrified to ring the bell. Instead, I sent a text.

hey i'm in front of your house

But before Earl came out, Maxwell wandered out onto the porch.

"Fuck you want," he said, although sort of casually and unthreateningly.

"I'm just waiting for Earl," I said, in my new loud middle-aged-Jewish-woman voice.

Earl appeared in the doorway.

"Sup," he said.

"Hey," I said.

We were sort of silent.

"You gonna come in?"

"No, I'm good," I heard myself say. I had rejected a normal invitation to go into his house. This made it clear that we were about to have an argument.

"O-*ho*," crowed Maxwell.

Earl went from Mega-Pissed to Genuinely Mega-Pissed and Not Just in Default Mode.

"The fuck's your problem," he spat.

"Uh, I was talking to Rachel, and she told me you told her about the, uh, the film."

All Earl said to that was "Yeah." Maybe he was just pretending that he didn't know this was a big deal. Maybe he was so pissed that he wasn't even registering it.

"It's just," I said, babbling, "you know, I mean, you told Rachel about the films in the first place, and then you brought them over to her, without asking me, and it's just like, you'll tell her anything, like, it doesn't even matter what I want, I'm not saying she shouldn't, she shouldn't know, or get to see them, I'm just saying, I wish you had *asked* me, first, I wish—"

"You know what? Just shut the fuck up. Shut the fuck up."

"I just—"

"I'm tired of this shit. I'm really fucking tired of it. You gotta quit with this shit, man. Because I'm about to lose my motherfucking shit with this."

Briefly I contemplated lecturing Earl about trust. I decided pretty quickly, however, that that was not going to work, and might also bring about the apocalypse. Also, it was becoming increasingly difficult for me to say words. Instead, I stood there and—there's no good way to put this—attempted not to cry.

"Naw, shut the fuck up. You care so fucking much bout what other people think, you gotta be secretive as shit, gotta go round sucking errybody's *dick* pretendin like you they friend cuz you care so much bout what they think, lemme fucking tell you: *Nobody gives a shit about you.* Nobody think shit about you. You ain't got no *friends.* You ain't *got* nobody who give a fucking shit about you."

"Oka , kay."

"Fuckin *nobody.* Errybody at school could give a *shit* about you, man. Errybody you all friendly with and shit could give a *shit.* You all worried bout what they think about you, man, they don't give a *fuck.* They don't give a fuck if you *live* or *die,* you pussy-ass bitch. They don't give a *fuck.* Look at me. They don't. Give. A *fuck.*"

"Oka ay. J Jesu , us."

"Man, just shut the fuck up, because I can't be hearing no more of this. Yeah, I fucking told Rachel about the films, I fucking gave her some of them dumb-ass films to watch, because she like the only person that *do* give a fuck. Yeah. She don't have big-ass titties, so you don't fucking care, but that other bitch don't give a shit about you and, and fucking Rachel *do,* and you don't fucking give a *shit* cuz you're a dumb little bitch."

"I d , d do."

"Stop your fucking crying, bitch-ass."

"O , Ok kay."

"Goddammit stop *cryin.*"

"OK."

Did I mention Maxwell was there for this? He was enjoying it. I am pretty sure his presence was making Earl more crazy and aggressive than he would have been normally.

"Now go on get the fuck outta here. I'm tired a lookin at your pussy ass. Crying and shit."

I didn't say anything or move. This caused Earl to get up in my face.

"God *damn* I'm sick and fucking tired a watchin you treat this girl like she some kind of, some kinda *burden,* when she the closest thing you fucking *have* to a motherfucking friend and she about to die on top of that. You know that, right? You dumb motherfucker. She home now cuz she *about to die.* That girl lyin there on her goddamn *deathbed* and you come to *my house* all whinin and cryin and shit about some irrelevant bullshit. I *want* . . . to kick your ass. You hear me? I *want* . . . to beat the *fuck* out of you right now."

"Go for it."

"You want me to?"

"I don't ca , care."

"Motherfucker, you *want* me to?"

I was in the middle of sarcastically but also tearfully saying,

"Yeah, Earl, I fucking want you to," when he punched me in the stomach.

So. There I was, for the second time in a month, lying in the Jackson front yard doubled over in pain, with a diminutive warlike kid standing over me. But this time at least it wasn't a kid with a socially unacceptable word tattooed on his neck. He also wasn't repeatedly slapping my face as I attempted to relearn how breathing works.

Instead, he was muttering things like, "Man, get up," and "I ain't even hit you for real."

Maxwell chimed in a few times with "Yeah! Hit him again!" and "BUST HIS CANDY ASS." But his heart wasn't really in it. I think he was disappointed that our fight was so lame. In fairness to us, the notion that we would have an interesting fight is absurd. It was like expecting a good fight between a wolverine and, I dunno, an animal made out of marshmallows.

Eventually, Maxwell went inside and it was just the two of us out there, and if Earl was still angry, it didn't seem to be at me.

"Goddamn, you a pussy. Get hit once in the gut, act like you dyin. Goddamn."

"Unngh."

"There you go. Walk it off, son."

"Jesus."

"Come on, let's go to your place. Get to work."

"Unnnh shit."

"That's right. Come on. I'll help you."

Chapter 35

DEADLINE

For Plan E we didn't even use Dad's camera. We used the low-quality camera on my laptop. We were inspired by YouTube. God help us.

Like whiny boring people all over the world, we decided that the best way of expressing ourselves was just to stare into the camera and talk. No script, no camera movement, no special lighting. We decided to strip all the effects away and see what was left.

Was this a terrible idea? Please stand by while I forward your question to the President of Yestonia.

```
INT. GREG'S ROOM — DAY


                    GREG
          So. Rachel.


                    EARL
          Sup Rachel.
```

                    GREG
We've tried, uh, a bunch of different
ways of making a film for you, and
uh, none of them have really turned
out the way we wanted.

If you don't script your dialogue, first of all, you're going to
pause and say "uh" at least a billion times. So for starters, you're
talking as though you've just suffered a semi-serious head injury.

                    EARL
We tried to do somethin with sock
puppets, and it didn't seem to be
very relevant to your, uh, situation.

                    GREG
Uh, we had everyone at school say
get-well wishes for the camera, but
uh, you've already had a bunch of
get-well cards, and we, uh, wanted
to do something more uh personal
than that.

                    EARL
We tried to do a documentary about
you. Uhh

GREG

Uhhhhh

EARL

There was a shortage of material,
to, uh, work with.

GREG

We tried this, uh, complicated stop-
motion, uh, animation thing, to get
you fired up about beating cancer,
but, uh. It ended up just really
goofy and, uh, not what we wanted.

EARL

So, now we're, uh, trying this.

BOTH

[garbled]

GREG

You go.

EARL

Naw, you go.

GREG

Just go.

                    EARL
         slowly, somehow painfully
Uh . . . All right. Uh. You probably
don't understand how grateful I am
to have gotten to know you. Because
first of all, the odds of that
happening, normally, would be very
low, because, speaking perfectly
honestly, we don't travel in the same
circles, you and me. So it feels like
. . . a blessing, to have had you in
my life these past few weeks.

I admire a lot of things about you.
I admire how smart you are, how
perceptive, and observant. But, uh.
What I'm just really in awe of, is
your, uh, I don't know how to put it.
I guess, your *patience*. If it was
me, I would be angry, and miserable,
and, and *hurtful*, and just terrible
to be around. And you've been so
strong throughout, and so *patient*,
even when things aren't going right,
and I'm in awe of that. And you've
made me feel, uh, blessed.
         finishing, husky-voiced
So, uh, yeah.

255

How the fuck was I supposed to follow that.

The basic problem was, Earl meant everything he said, and I couldn't say the same stuff without lying. Because Earl is just a better person than me. I don't want to sound like a melodramatic jackass, but that's the truth. I was pretty sure I couldn't say *anything* sensitive, and reassuring, and touching, without it being a lie.

```
                    EARL (CONT'D)
              choked up and now sort of angry
        Your turn.
```

Was Rachel inspiring to me? Did I really think she was smart, and perceptive, and patient, and everything else? No. I'm sorry. Look: I feel terrible. I wish that getting to know her had been this big inspiring life-improving thing. I really do. I know that's what's supposed to happen. But it *didn't*.

```
                    EARL (CONT'D)
        Dude. It's your turn.
```

So what was I supposed to say? The truth?

```
                    EARL (CONT'D)
              punching Greg in the arm
        Your turn, jackass.
```

GREG

Right. Right right. Uh. The main
reason we made this video is, uh.
We want you to get better. And, uh.
Look. The thing is: I *know* you can
get better. I know you're strong
enough, and, uh. Yeah. I just wanted
to tell you. Uh. I believe in you.
> *talking maybe a little too much
> now*

And that's, uh, I realize now, that's
why we wanted to make a film. To tell
you that we believe in you.
> *just really driving the lie
> home at this point*

And that's why we, uh, made the film.

I spent an entire weekend listening to myself say "we believe in you," and wanting to punch myself in the face. Because it was such an obvious lie. If we really believed in Rachel, we wouldn't be rushing to make this film before she died. Plus, I mean, why the hell would we believe in her? She didn't even believe in herself. She told me point-blank she thought she was going to die. She was stopping treatment and going home and waiting for the inevitable. Who were we to argue with that?

At the same time, there wasn't really anything else to say.

Mom walked into the computer room late Sunday night.

"Honey."

"Oh, hey."

"Are you still working on the movie for Rachel?"

"Yeah."

"How's it going."

"'Sgoing fine."

"Oh honey. Shhhhh."

"'*Sfine.*"

"Shhhhhhhh."

"h hurnk."

"It's hard to lose a friend."

"Tha , at's, snot it."

"It's hard, honey."

"That's not , n not , , it."

"Shhhh."

Chapter 36

RACHEL THE FILM

Rachel the Film (dir. G. Gaines and E. Jackson, 2011). This film, a loose homage to leukemia victim Rachel Kushner, is perhaps most noteworthy for its confusing mishmash of styles, incorporating documentary footage, confessionals, stop-motion animation, and puppetry in what can only be thought of as a huge mess. In fact, directors Gaines and Jackson begin the film with a grainy, pixilated apology to Rachel herself, admitting that the film is badly organized and basically incoherent. After that comes a pastiche of awkward well-wishes from high school students and teachers, sock puppets hitting each other, LEGO characters with incomprehensible accents, poorly scanned photos of Kushner's childhood, and other absurdist one-offs with extremely limited relevance to the subject matter. The weepy, melodramatic conclusion, again featuring the directors, is frankly unwatchable. It is, however, a fitting end to what is almost certainly the worst film ever made. ★

The last time I talked to Rachel, she had seen *Rachel the Film* a few times, and I wasn't sure how to talk to her about it. She was in bed, as usual, but not wearing her hat. She sounded the same as ever: kind of scraggly-voiced and congested in the nose. It occurred to me for the first time that that's maybe what I sound like a little bit, too.

"Hey," I said.

"Hey," she said.

For some reason I wanted to go in for a fist pound, but I didn't.

"I saw *Rachel the Film*," she said.

"Mmmm."

"I liked it."

"You know you really don't have to say that."

"No, I did like it."

"Uh, if you're sure."

"I mean, it's probably not my *favorite*."

It was somehow a big relief that she was honest about it. I don't know why this relieved me. I think I might have a disorder where your emotions frequently malfunction and a lot of the time you're sitting there feeling something inappropriate. It should be called Emotional Moron Disorder.

"Yeah, if it was your favorite, that would mean you had kind of questionable taste, because it's really not very good."

"It's good, it's just not as good as some of the others."

"No, seriously. I don't know what happened. We worked insanely hard on it, and then, I don't know. We just couldn't do it."

"You guys did fine."

"No, we *didn't*."

I wanted to explain to her why things had gone so horribly wrong, but obviously I didn't *know* why. I mean, Earl and I are not expert filmmakers, but at this point in our careers we should be creating something better than the sickening depressing chaos that is *Rachel the Film.*

"You're funny," she said. She had a bigger smile on her face than I had seen in a while.

"What?"

"You're so hard on yourself. It's funny."

"I'm hard on myself because I'm a jackass."

"No you're not."

"No, you have no idea."

Maybe I couldn't explain how we had made the Worst Film in the Entire World. But I *could* talk some trash on myself! I'm starting to realize that this is my favorite thing.

"No, you don't have to live inside my head. For every, just, insanely stupid thing I do or say, there are like fifty even worse ones that I just barely avoid doing or saying, just out of dumb luck."

"Greg."

"I'm serious."

"I'm happy we became friends again."

"Oh yeah? I mean, yeah. I mean, me, too."

And then we sat and didn't say anything for a while. You're probably hoping that I was sitting there overflowing with love

and tenderness. Maybe you should think about switching to a different book. Even to, like, an owner's manual to a refrigerator or something. That would be more heartwarming than this.

Because mostly I was feeling resentful and annoyed. I was resentful at Rachel for deciding to die. How stupid does that sound? There's a decent chance that I'm not even a human being. Anyway, yeah, I was pissed that she was just going to go die. And I was maybe even more pissed that I had felt manipulated into pretending, in *Rachel the Film*, like I thought she wasn't. I had looked into the camera and said, "I *know* you can get better," and "I believe in you." You could even see in my stupid eyes that I didn't believe what I was saying. There was no way to edit that to make it look any other way. And obviously I'm a colossal jackass, but it *was* also Rachel who put me in that stupid position, by giving up on her entire life and leaving everyone else to pretend that it wasn't happening.

Maybe Rachel sensed that I was thinking about the film, because she brought it up again.

"It was really nice of you to do that film."

"Well, it sucked, but we had to do it. There's no good reason why it's not better."

"You didn't have to do it!"

Rachel was sort of wide-eyed.

"Yeah, we did."

"No."

"You're literally our only fan. We had to make something for you."

"Well, actually, there is something I want you do for me."

This was so unexpected that I was able to make a joke.

"But we already made you a film! *Is there no end to your demands, tyrant.* TYRANT WOMAN."

There was some weak snorting and giggling. Then it seemed like she had to compose herself before talking again.

"I went through that college book."

"Oh yeah?"

"Yeah. And I found some film schools in there."

It took me a surprisingly long time to get the point of what she was talking about.

"I also found some other colleges with good film programs," she said.

I was nodding my head stupidly. I knew I couldn't argue with any of this.

"I want you to take your films and apply to them. Earl, too."

"Uh, OK."

"That's the only thing I want you to do."

"Yeah."

"Can you do that?"

"Yeah, sure."

"You promise."

"Yeah, I promise."

Chapter 37

THE ENDS OF OUR LIVES

So. I'm finally getting to the part where my life gets ruined by Mom, and also Earl's life. Go get some popcorn! This is gonna be awesome. I'll wait right here.

Mmmm. Buttery, salty popcorn.

Actually, I'm gonna go make some popcorn, too. Hang on.

Fuck, this is the diet kind. This is disgusting. This tastes like the inside of a couch.

Fuckburglar.

So in the making of *Rachel the Film,* I fell behind on schoolwork sort of a lot. I already kind of told you about that, but during *Rachel the Film,* things reached sort of an embarrassing point. Basically, I was getting gangbanger-level grades, and teachers were starting to take me aside after class to tell me that I was destroying my own life. And finally, the day after I delivered the one copy of *Rachel the Film* to Rachel, Mr. McCarthy staged an intervention. He went to Mom and Dad, and the three of them agreed that Mr. McCarthy was allowed to keep me after school every day for hours to prevent me from failing my classes.

Did this happen to Earl? No. Earl takes classes where you don't fail, period. It doesn't matter what work you do or how often you show up. You could staple a dead animal to your homework and you wouldn't fail. You could show up one day and pelt your teacher with bags of narcotics and poop. They'd probably just send you to the vice principal's office or something.

So suddenly I was doing schoolwork all the time, under the watchful, quietly insane eye of Mr. McCarthy. I guess I was actually sort of grateful that someone else was taking over my life. I mean, I'm obviously pretty terrible at managing my own life, so it was nice to know that it was in good hands. But also it was nice to have all these concrete tasks to do and be sort of distracted and consumed by them. It kept me from thinking about every depressing weird thing that was going on at that time.

Unfortunately, it also prevented me from noticing that Mom was suddenly behaving abnormally.

Normally, when I'm home, she likes to do some annoying check-in at least every hour. There is no end to the reasons moms can use for annoying check-ins.

- Just seeing how things are going
- Just seeing if you need any help with anything
- Just wanted to say it's a beautiful day outside and maybe you should think about getting some exercise
- Just letting you know that I'm going to spin class

- Just letting you know I'm back from spin class
- Just letting you know that Gretchen is being A Little Difficult Right Now so please don't aggravate her
- Just wondering if you want beef tips for dinner or do you eat lamb because I was heading out to Whole Foods but I forget if you eat lamb
- Just had a question for you but now I forget what it is, so I'll just ask you later, unless you might know what the question was, but you probably don't, so I'll just come back later, so things are going OK? They are? Honey, you need to turn some lights on in here or you'll destroy your eyes

For a few days, this came to an unprecedented halt. I wasn't home as much, and then when I was home, there were no check-ins. In hindsight, I really should have suspected something was up. But I was busy, and also, I was probably unconsciously grateful for the temporary lack of annoying check-ins, and unwilling to risk re-triggering them.

The hammer fell during eighth period.

One great thing about eighth-period lunch is that pep rallies are always scheduled for eighth period, so Earl and I never have to go to them. However, at least in theory, they're mandatory attendance for the whole school, and for some reason Mr. McCarthy was a jerk about this one.

"Sorry, guys," he said, standing in the doorway as his ninth-grade history class milled around outside like disoriented toddlers. "I'd get in big trouble if anyone found you here during the pep rally."

So we left our lunches on his desk and tagged along with the ninth graders to the auditorium.

For most pep rallies, the marching band's drum section is onstage, pounding out some repetitive beat, and maybe some of the bolder athletes grab a microphone and try to freestyle over it, until they get too sexually explicit or accidentally say the F- or N-word, at which point a vice principal shuts them down. However, there was just a massive projector screen onstage, and no drummers; just Principal Stewart. We were among the last classes to arrive, and so we had barely sat down among the ninth graders when Principal Stewart took the microphone and spoke.

Principal Stewart is a giant, terrifying black man. There's no other way to put it. He is extremely authoritative, and his default facial expression, like Earl's, is Pissed. I had never been directly addressed by him, and I was hoping to keep it that way until graduation.

His speaking style is hard to describe. There's sort of an angry undercurrent to everything he says, even when the words aren't angry at all, and there are a lot of pauses. He definitely sounded pissed at the pep rally.

"Students and teachers. Of Benson High School. Welcome to this pep rally. We are here. To cheer the Trojans. To certain victory over Allderdice. Tonight on the football field."

Cheering and hollering that Principal Stewart, glaring at all of us, brought to an abrupt end.

"However. It is for a *greater purpose*. That I have assembled

everyone. Here on this afternoon. I will make my words brief. On this subject."

Major pause.

"A member of the Benson family. Is in the fight of her life. Against cancer. You may know her personally. And if not you have certainly heard. Her name. Her name is Rachel Kushner. We have *all*. At one time or another. Sent our prayers. Out to her and her family. They are needed."

The anger sort of made this sound ironic, which made me sort of giggle quietly. And then Principal Stewart was staring right at me, and I had this dumb smile frozen on my face, and words cannot describe to you the terror I felt at that moment.

"But two students. Have gone further. Much further. They have spent countless hours. Creating a film."

Next to me, I heard Earl make a strangled noise.

"A film to lift Rachel's spirits. A film to give her company. And hope. And love. A film to make her laugh. And feel cherished."

For every word that Principal Stewart was saying, I wanted to punch myself in the face.

"They did not intend. For anyone but Rachel. To see this film. They did this for her. And her alone. However, gestures of love. Of this quality. Are surely worth seeing. And appreciating. And applauding."

A new feeling came over me. I wanted to punch myself in the *junk*.

"Gregory Gaines. Earl Jackson. Please come to the stage."

My legs felt weak. I couldn't stand up. The back of my throat tasted like barf. Earl had a look on his face like a dead man. I was trying to black out on command. I wasn't quite able to do it.

What had happened was, Denise had found the film. Rachel had put it on and then fallen asleep. And Denise walked into the room, found it, and watched it. And then Denise shared it with Mom. And Mom told Denise about how Earl and I never let anyone see anything. And Denise and Mom decided that *everyone* should see this film. And without letting us know, they went to some teachers at the school. And the teachers saw it. And Principal Stewart saw it. And now everyone was about to see it.

Onstage, as people halfheartedly applauded, Principal Stewart clapped his giant hands on our shoulders, glared at us as though he was about to eat our flesh, and said quietly, "I am very moved. By what you boys have done. You are a credit to this school." Then the three of us sat in chairs off to one side, and Earl's giant head and my somehow even gianter head appeared on the screen, and for twenty-eight minutes, everyone at Benson sat through *Rachel the Film.*

Chapter 38

AFTERMATH

So. If this was some normal fictional young-adult book, this is the part of the story where after the film, the entire high school would rise to their feet and applaud, and Earl and I would find True Acceptance and begin to Truly Believe in Ourselves, and Rachel would somehow miraculously make a recovery, or maybe she would die but we would Always Have Her to Thank for Making Us Discover Our Inner Talent, and Madison would become my girlfriend and I would get to nuzzle her boobs like an affectionate panda cub whenever I wanted.

That is why fiction sucks. None of that happened. Instead, pretty much everything happened that I was afraid of, except worse.

1. My Classmates Did Not Particularly Enjoy *Rachel the Film*

They hated it. They thought it was weird and confusing. They also thought we had forced them to watch it, despite what Principal Stewart said. Most students weren't paying very close attention to his speech. They just showed up at the auditorium, started paying attention when the lights went down, and assumed that it was *our* idea to make everyone watch the stupid film. And because it genuinely sucks, they hated it. Earl and I got to watch their reactions from onstage. There was a lot of restless fidgeting, bored conversations, teachers hissing "Shhh," and hostile glaring. So that wasn't great.

The worst part was the occasional screams of outrage. The spinning tarantula, for example, caused more than a couple of people to lose their shit. "That ain't right!" "That's *nasty.*" "WHY WE GOTTA WATCH THIS."

Actually, maybe it was worse to see the reactions of Rachel's friends Anna and Naomi. They both clearly hated it. Naomi made her feelings clear by having an enormous scowl on her face and rolling her eyes roughly every ten seconds. And the thing was, I couldn't even really blame her for that. Anna was worse, because she just looked kind of miserable. She was being comforted by Scott Mayhew, the guy who I pretended was a barfing alien. He had become her boyfriend. Scott was mostly glaring at me, with the icy unblinking hatred of a gothy dork who feels that his trust has been betrayed. I guess I was lucky that he didn't have a sword.

The teachers all made a big deal of liking it, which (1) reflects poorly on their artistic judgment and (2) made the students hate it even more. It kept getting rubbed in everyone's face that we had done this stupid film. It started to look as though we had just done it because we wanted attention. That idea, of course, makes me want to throw poisonous stinging insects at my own head.

Some of the stoners liked it, and that did not make me feel better about anything. Dave Smeggers, for example, stopped me in the hall to tell me that he thought the film was "deep."

"It was *funny*, man," he said. "You took death, like a real person's death, and you made it *funny*. You made it funny as hell! That blew me away."

It didn't seem worth it to tell him that that actually wasn't our goal.

Madison claimed to like it, but it was pretty obvious she was just being nice. The kicker was when she said she didn't understand all of it.

"You guys are just so *creative*," she explained, as though that permitted us to make any weird, alienating, poorly created thing and force people to watch it.

So everyone saw it. Almost everyone hated it.

In the words of Nizar the Surly Syrian, "You want to fight, I fight you. Cock shit ass fuck."

2. My Classmates Now Had Active Reason to Dislike Me

And so in the days directly after the screening of *Rachel the Film*, my role in the Benson ecosystem changed again, for the worse. At the beginning of the year I had been Greg Gaines, the guy who is casually friendly with everyone. Then I became Greg Gaines, Possible Boyfriend of a Boring Girl. That wasn't great; nor was Greg Gaines, Filmmaker. But now I was Greg Gaines, Filmmaker Who Specifically Makes Shitty Experimental Films and Forces You to Watch Them. I was a lone chimp, hobbling around on the forest floor. I also had a ginormous target on the back of my head and a sign under it that said: "Betcha Can't Hit My Head with Your Thrown Feces!"

I couldn't even bring myself to talk to anyone at school. I wasn't able to talk to anyone anyway, without it being film-related. Kids would shout things at me in the hall from time to time—often about the spinning tarantula, which I think really came to symbolize the film's aggressive awfulness—and I was unable to come up with a response that would make it OK. Instead, I would just kind of walk faster. This felt horrible.

In terms of social groups: The smart kids treated me with outright pity. The rich kids suddenly behaved as though they had never known me. The jocks started asking me when I was going to do a gay porn. The theater kids—this was the worst—seemed to think that, now that I had invaded their auditorium, we had some kind of tense artistic rivalry going. And most other kids just treated me with a combination of mistrust and dislike.

So that wasn't great.

3. Earl and I Stayed Far, Far Away from Each Other

We had no interest in hanging out. None.

4. I Had Kind of a Meltdown and Became a Hermit

In fairness, I definitely did not react very well to what happened. The screening was in December, so I went to school for another week after that, and then the week before winter break, I just sort of stopped going to school. I biked to Home Depot, bought a lock for my door, attached it kind of messily with some power tools, and locked myself in my room.

Since the film thing, the only parent I was on speaking terms with was Dad, and even then I didn't really want to talk to him, so instead we sent texts to each other. It was weird.

Son, Are you going to school today?

no

Why not?

feel sick

Should we take you to a doctor?

no i just need to be alone

So you don't have a broken arm or anything?

why would i have a broken arm

You don't really know how to use power tools! LOL

no broken arm

Well, feel free to make lunch for yourself in the kitchen. I'll be in my study if you need anything.

I learned later that Mom was so upset about this whole fiasco that she let Dad talk her into being much more hands-off with me than before. This, of course, was completely welcome by me. In fact, Mom finally staying out of my life was probably the only thing that prevented me from attempting to jog to Buenos Aires.

So for a week I just stayed in my room and watched films. First I watched only the good ones, in the hopes that they would cheer me up, but all they did was remind me of what a terrible filmmaker I was. Then I watched some bad films, but that didn't make me feel good, either. Every now and then I put in a Gaines/Jackson DVD, and had to take it out after five minutes. Our films were just so bad. They just were. We didn't have any equipment, or actors. We were just kids making embarrassing kid stuff. I put in the ones I thought would be the best, and they were terrible. *Star Peaces. 2002. Cat-ablanca.* Horrific. An abomination. Boring, stupid, unwatchable.

And on Day Three I freaked out and took out a scissors and scratched them all up and threw them in the garbage, and I knew at the time it wasn't going to make me feel any better, but I did it anyway, because, fuck it.

So I was feeling about as awful as I had ever felt when Dad called my cell phone one afternoon to tell me that Rachel was back in the hospital.

Chapter 39

AFTERMATH II

Denise was there when I got to Rachel's room, and we didn't really have anything to say to each other, so we both awkwardly sat there for a while. I felt like I should leave, but I knew that would make me feel even worse. Rachel wasn't awake. She had pneumonia, apparently.

I really wanted Rachel to wake up. In retrospect, this was stupid and pointless, because I had nothing to say to her, but I just wanted to talk to her again. I sat there staring at her for like an hour. Her frizzy hair was gone, and her mouth was closed, so I couldn't see her sort of big teeth. And her eyes were closed, so I couldn't see them, either. So you'd think the person lying there wouldn't have looked like Rachel at all, but somehow she did.

Actually I was crying the whole time, because for some reason it had never really sunk in with me that she was dying, and now I was literally watching her die, and it was different somehow.

There was just something about her dying that I had understood but not *really* understood, if you know what I mean.

I mean, you can know someone is dying on an intellectual level, but emotionally it hasn't really hit you, and then when it does, that's when you feel like shit.

So like an idiot, I hadn't understood until I was sitting there actually watching her physically die, when it was too late to say or do anything. I couldn't believe it had taken me so long to understand it even a little bit. This was a human being, dying. This was the only time there was going to be someone with *those* eyes and *those* ears and *that* way of breathing through her mouth and *that* way of building up right before a monster laugh with her eyebrows all raised and her nostrils flaring a little bit, this was the only time there was ever going to be that person, living in the world, and now that was almost over, and I couldn't deal with it.

I was thinking, also, that we had made a film about a thing, death, that we knew nothing about. Maybe Earl sort of knew something, but I knew absolutely *nothing* about it. Plus we had made a film about a girl who we really hadn't gotten to know. Actually, we hadn't made the film about her at all. She was just dying, there, and we had gone and made a film about ourselves. We had taken this girl and used her really to make a film about *ourselves*, and it just seemed so stupid and wrong that I couldn't stop crying. *Rachel the Film* is not at all about Rachel. It's about how little we know about Rachel. We were so ridiculously arrogant to try to make a film about her.

So I was sitting there and the whole time I had this insane wish for Rachel to wake up and just tell me everything she had ever thought, so that it could be recorded somewhere, so that it wouldn't be lost. I found myself thinking, what if she's already

had her last thought, what if her brain isn't producing conscious thoughts anymore, and that was so awful that I started completely bawling, I was making hideous sobbing noises like an elephant seal or something, like: HURNK HURNGK HRUNNNN.

Denise was just sitting there frozen.

At the same time, and I hated myself for this, I was realizing how to make the movie I should have made, that it had to be something that stored as much of Rachel as possible, that ideally we *would* have had a camera on her for her whole life, and one inside her head, and it made me so bitter and fucking angry that this was impossible, and she was just going to be *lost*. Just as if she had never been around to say things and laugh at people and have favorite words that she liked to use and ways of fidgeting with her fingers when she got antsy and specific memories that flashed through her head when she ate a certain food or smelled a certain smell like, I dunno, how maybe honeysuckle made her think of one particular summer day playing with a friend or whatever the fuck, or how rain on the windshield of her mom's car used to look like alien fingers to her, or *whatever*, and as if she had never had fantasies about stupid Hugh Jackman or visions of what her life was going to be like in college or a whole unique way of thinking about the world that was never going to be articulated to anyone. All of it and everything else she had ever thought was just going to be lost.

And the point of *Rachel the Film* should really have been to express how awful and shitty that loss was, that she would have become a person with a long awesome life if she had been allowed to continue living, and that this was just a stupid meaningless *loss*, just a motherfucking *loss*, a loss loss loss fucking loss, there was no fucking meaning to it, there was nothing good that could come out of it, and I was sitting there thinking about the film and I knew the film would have to have a scene of me losing my shit in the hospital room, and her mom sitting there wordless and dead-eyed like a statue, and I hated myself for having a cold detached part of me that thought this, but I couldn't help it.

At some point during all this, my mom came in, and if you think it was possible for either of us to talk through all the crying, you may just be stupid.

We had to step out into the hall eventually, but not before Mom had a bizarre interaction with Denise, where she hugged Denise's body and said some incoherent things while Denise just sat there rigidly.

So Mom and I sat there in two generic institutional chairs in the hallway and tried to get all the crying out of our system, and eventually I was able to talk in short little bursts.

"I just w want her to w , wake up."

"Oh, honey."

"It s sucks."

"You made her very happy."

"If I m , made her h happy, then why is sn' sn't she trying to f fight. Harder."

"It's just too hard. Honey. Some things, *no one* can fight."

"It *sucks*."

"Death happens to everyone."

"HurrnNRNNNGK."

This went on for like an hour. I'll spare you the rest of it. Eventually, we stopped talking, and there was a long silence as people like Gilbert were wheeled around and doctors and nurses strode briskly past them.

Then Mom said: "I'm sorry."

I thought I knew what she was talking about.

"Well, I just wish you had asked me first."

"I *did* ask you first, but I guess I didn't really give you a choice."

"Mom, what are you talking about. You didn't ask me first."

"Are we talking about the same thing?"

"I'm talking about the stupid pep rally."

"Oh."

"What are you talking about."

"*I'm* talking about getting you to spend time with Rachel in the first place."

"The pep rally was way worse."

"That, I don't feel bad about. I *do* feel bad about making you deal with such a difficul—"

"You don't feel bad about the pep rally?"

"No, but I do feel bad ab—"

"The pep rally was a nightmare. It was literally like a nightmare."

"If you *regret* that your beautiful movie was shown to your classmates, then I really don't know how to respond to that."

"I can't believe that you still think that was a *good idea*. First of all, th—"

"There are some things—"

"Can I just finish?"

"First, there are some—"

"Can I just *finish*. Mom. Mom, let me finish. *Mom.* Jesus *Christ.*"

We were both using Mom's unstoppable nonstop-stream-of-words move, and I think she was so surprised that I was using it back on her that she actually relented and let me talk.

"Fine. What."

"Mom. My classmates hated the film. And Earl and I really don't like it either. We don't think it's very good. In fact, we think it's terrible."

"If you—"

"Mom, you have to let me finish."

"Fine."

"It's not a good film. OK? Actually, it sucks. Because—Mom, *chill*—we had pretty good intentions, but that doesn't mean we made a good film. OK? Because it's not about her at all. It's just this embarrassing thing that shows that we don't even understand anything about her. And also, you're my mom, so you're ridiculously biased, and you can't see that the film actually sucks and doesn't make any sense."

"Honey. It's so *creative*. It—"

"Just because something is weird and hard to understand doesn't mean it's *creative*. That's—that's the whole problem. If you want to pretend like something is good, even when it's not, that's when you use the stupid word 'creative.' The film sucked. Our classmates hated it."

"They just didn't understand it."

"They didn't understand it because we made a *shitty film*."

"Honey."

"If it was good, they would have liked it. They would have understood it. And if it was good, maybe it would have helped."

We were quiet again. Someone a few doors down seemed to be loudly dying. It really did not help the mood.

"Well, maybe you're right."

"I *am* right."

"Well, I'm sorry."

"OK."

"What you don't understand is, it's hard when your children start growing up," said Mom, and all of a sudden she was crying again, way harder than before, and I had to comfort her. We were doing a Cross-Chair Hug, and physically it was extremely awkward.

Crying semi-hysterically, Mom made a number of points:

- Your friend is dying
- It's just so hard to watch a child die
- And it's much harder to watch a friend's daughter die
- But the hardest is watching your son watching his friend die
- You have to make your own decisions now
- It's so hard for me to let you make your own decisions
- But I have to let you make your own decisions

- I am so proud of you
- Your friend is dying, and you have been so strong

I wanted to argue with some of this. I hadn't been strong at all, and I definitely didn't feel like I had done anything to be proud of. But somehow I knew this was no time for an episode of *Excessive Modesty Hour*.

We left. I knew I wouldn't see Rachel again. I just felt kind of empty and exhausted. Mom got me some Kahlúa ice cream with habaneros and bee pollen in it. It tasted OK.

That's when I knew I was going to make it.

Chapter 40

AFTERMATH III

Winter break was almost over. It hadn't snowed yet. Earl and I were in Thuyen's Saigon Flavor and it was the first time we had seen each other since I became a hermit. Thuyen's Saigon Flavor is that Vietnamese restaurant in Lawrenceville that Mr. McCarthy recommended to us the day we accidentally got stoned and told Rachel that we were filmmakers. I thought Earl would be more likely to want to meet up if it was at a place with bizarre and possibly inedible food.

Earl was already there when I showed up. I was sweating a lot under my winter coat because I had biked from my house. Also, my glasses were all fogged up, so I had to take them off and squint around like a mole-rat. Earl did not identify himself, so I wandered at random around the restaurant until I located him. He was sullenly stirring his bowl of soup.

"WELCOME WELCOME," said a blurry object who was probably Thuyen, momentarily scaring the hell out of me.

"Hey," I said to Earl.

"Sup."

"Is that pho?"

"Yeah."

"Is it good?"

"It's got tendons in it and shit."

"Huh."

"WHAT YOU LIKE TO ORDER," said Thuyen. He was about my height and shape, and he seemed disproportionately happy that we were there.

"Pho," I said.

"ONE PHO," bellowed Thuyen, and waddled away.

"Drug-free for once," muttered Earl.

The music was extremely smooth R&B, and it was playing kind of loud. "You're my sexy love," a guy was crooning. "Se-e-exy lo-o-ove."

"So," I said. "I dunno if you heard, but Rachel died."

"Yeah, I heard."

"So, uh. Did you end up getting your DVDs back from her?"

"Yeah," said Earl, stirring.

"Can we make some copies of those?"

Earl raised his eyebrows.

"I sort of freaked out," I said. "I kind of had this freak-out and, uh, scratched all my copies up. So I don't have any copies anymore."

Earl looked at me kind of bug-eyed.

"I *burnt* mine," he said.

"Oh," I said. For some reason, this didn't surprise me all that much. I probably should have freaked out when I heard it.

"Yeah," he said. "I burnt em in a trash can."

"I guess there are no more copies," I said.

"You jacked yours up? They don't play no more?"

"Yeah," I said.

"Damn," Earl said.

"Ooh girl!" bleated the R&B guy. "You make me say, 'Ooh ooh ooh.'"

We were both quiet for a while. Then Earl said, "I didn't think you was gonna jack up your copies."

"Yeah," I said. "I just kind of freaked out. I dunno."

"It didn't even *occur* to me that you would . . . do something like that."

"I shouldn't have done it," I said, but Earl didn't seem to be trying to make me feel bad. He just seemed kind of astonished.

"ONE PHO," announced Thuyen, putting the bowl on the table. It smelled kind of great and kind of nasty. I would be smelling it and it would have this amazing kind of beefy sweet licorice smell for a while, and then suddenly there would be this hint of some other smell, which was sort of the smell of a sweaty butt. There was also a big complicated plate with leaves and fruit and sperm-looking bean sprouts on it.

I was trying to figure out what to eat first when Earl suddenly said, "It's a good thing, man, because I can't be making films no more. I gotta get a job or something. I gotta make some money and get outta my mom's goddamn house."

"Oh yeah?" I said.

"Yeah," said Earl. "It's time to move on, man. I can't be doing this no more."

"What kind of job are you thinking about getting?"

"Man, I don't know. Manage a Wendy's or some shit."

We tried to eat. The broth was OK. The various animal parts were a little too weird for me. They had little knobbly bumps and huge chunks of fat and stuff. There were also "beef balls." There was no way I was going to eat those.

I don't know why I brought it up, but I said, "I'm probably failing some classes."

"Yeah?"

"Yeah, I stopped going to school basically."

"Yup, McCarthy was pissed."

"Well, he can suck it," I said, and then was immediately filled with regret.

"Don't talk shit," said Earl.

I didn't say anything to that.

"You're stupid if you fail," continued Earl. He didn't sound pissed. He was being very matter-of-fact. "You're smarter than that, man. You got college and shit to look forward to. Get a good job and shit."

"I was thinking," I said, "maybe I don't want to go to college. Maybe I want to go to film school."

"What, cuz of Rachel."

"No. Did she say anything to you about film school?"

"She axed *me* to apply to film school. I figured she probly axed you, too. I was like, Girl, are you outta your mind. I ain't got no money for no film school."

"You could get a scholarship, though."

"Ain't nobody giving my ass no scholarship," said Earl, and finally he ate some noodles.

"Why not?" I asked.

Sort of menacingly, with his mouth full, Earl said, "It's just not gonna *happen*."

We ate some more. The R&B guy was singing happily about how a girl kept him "sprung." Thuyen was kind of singing along to it, from behind a sketchy-looking glass counter.

For some reason, I couldn't drop the film school thing.

"I'm probably gonna apply to film school anyway," I said. "So I guess I'll need to make some new films for that."

Earl was munching something.

"I don't know if you wanna help out with it," I said.

Earl didn't look at me. After a while he said, kind of sadly, "I can't be *doing* this anymore."

Then some kind of very evil and/or stupid space alien took control of my brain and made me say something unbelievably shitty.

"Rachel would probably like that, though," I heard myself say. "If we were working together."

Earl stared at me for a while.

"You don't know shit, man," he said finally. He was brisk and sad at the same time. "I hate to get on you for this. I'm *not* getting on you for this, but I'm just telling you. This is the first . . . *negative* thing that happened to you in your life. And you can't be overreacting to it and making big-ass expensive decisions based on it. I'm just saying. People die. Other people do stupid shit. I'm *surrounded* by family members doing stupid shit. I used a think I had to do shit for them. I still *wanna* do shit for them. But you gotta live your own life. You gotta take care a your *own shit* before you get started doing things for errybody else."

I was quiet because this was a completely unprecedented outburst for him. I mean, it was unprecedented because it was so personal. Or maybe that's not it. I don't know. Anyway, I was silenced by this and eventually that made him keep talking.

"I don't wanna leave my mama *behind*," he said, in the same tone of voice as before. "In that *house*. Drinking morning till night and always being online and shit. I don't wanna leave Derrick and Devin. They a couple of jackasses. They all dumb as hell, man. I look around and ain't nobody got a family as bad as mine. Ain't nobody live in a damn shithole of a house like mine.

"But I gotta take care of *my own shit*," he said. I think he was talking more to himself than to me at that point. He was sort of explaining, sort of pleading. "They got shit to figure out before I can help em. I love my mama, but she has problems that I can't help her with. I love my brothers, but they need to figure they shit out before I can help em. Otherwise they just gonna drag me down."

It was possible for me to go for months without remembering that Earl had a mom. It was really jarring for me to hear about her, for some reason. I didn't even have a picture of her in my head. She was this kind of small faded-looking woman with big eyes and a sort of dreamy smile all the time.

Anyway, Earl seemed happier that he had said all of this. Then he noticed me like he had forgotten that I was there.

"Same thing with you and Rachel, except she dead, so it don't even matter what you do for her. You gotta do what's good

for you. You gotta *graduate*, son. Graduate, go to college, get some job. We can't be doin this no more."

This was simultaneously awesome and depressing. At any rate, Earl had actually gotten himself in a good mood.

"The hell Vietnamese people even think to put some of this shit in soup," he said. "Look at this damn thing. Look like somebody's nutsack up in here."

Without warning, it was time for Gross-Out Mode. I didn't feel up to it, but I did my best.

"That's nutsack? That's not a butthole?"

"This wrinkly bullshit? Nutsack. I *think*. Check the menu."

"What about this thing with the fringe on it?"

"*That* might be a butthole. Did you order the large? The large got butthole, nutsack, uh, sautéed donkey dick, and uh, you probably got some hairy-ass goat titties floating around in there."

"Yeah, this is the large."

"Goat titties are rich in antioxidants."

"I'm looking for the donkey dick. I'm not seeing any donkey dick."

"Looks like you didn't get none."

"This is an outrage. There's no donkey dick in my soup. I'm so pissed about this."

"I most definitely had a couple generous chunks of finely sautéed donkey dick up in mine."

I sort of got burned out and couldn't add anything after a while.

"Don't be pissed, son," said Earl reassuringly. "I've had better."

EPILOGUE

So it's June and I just finished writing about all this. First of all: Thank Christ that this book is over. Also, I can probably just write whatever on this page, because there's no way you made it all the way to the end, because this book is a disgrace to the English language. To *all* language. They should take away my language privileges. But meanwhile, I can write anything I want. For example: Will Carruthers's penis is basically an innie. Suck it, Will Carruthers. I no longer care about being your friend.

So as you probably know, I got into Pitt, but then my admission was suspended when I failed the first semesters of English 12, Calculus I, Biology II, and gym. And Dad thought maybe it would make a difference if I explained to the admissions people at Pitt *why* I failed those classes. Dad kept throwing around the word "bereavement," which sounds like the word for being attacked by beavers. Mom thought I should show you *Rachel the Film*, and it is perhaps a sign of maturity that this suggestion didn't make me pretend to be dead even for like five

seconds. Then Mom and Dad suggested I make some kind of film for your special consideration, but after *Rachel the Film*, and after I found Earl was done with filmmaking, I retired from filmmaking forever.

But I thought about it and it did seem like I should try to explain myself in some way. And I haven't had anything to do this summer besides take these stupid makeup classes to get my degree. And I figured, anyone can write a book. So I wrote this book for you, Pitt admissions people. If nothing else, it should prove that actually *not* anyone can write a book, unless we're talking about a record-settingly inane book, so at least it's useful for that.

But now that I've written it, it's pretty obvious that this book is not going to change your mind. I mean, if it *does* change your mind and you decide to readmit me, then you guys should all be fired, because all I've really demonstrated to you is that I'm a jackass who doesn't feel appropriate emotions and can't really live a normal human life.

Also I think at some point I insulted your school by calling it the bigger, dumber sibling of Carnegie Mellon.

But writing this page right now, I just realized that I should un-retire as a filmmaker. So if you still want to take me, that's great. But just know that I'll probably be leaving in a year to apply for film school. So I'm gonna go start making films now. Maybe I'll even try to get some actors to be in them.

I've also had kind of a realization about myself and I might as well share it because no one is reading this. This book probably makes it seem like I hate myself and everything I do. But that's not totally true. I mostly just hate every person I've ever *been*. I'm actually fine with myself right now. I feel like there's a good chance I might make a really good film. One day. Probably in six months I will have changed my mind about that, but whatever. That is just part of the action-packed roller-coaster ride that is the life of Greg S. Gaines.

(Although let me also say this: Just because I'm un-retired doesn't mean I'll be making a film out of this book. There is no way in hell that is going to happen. When you convert a *good* book to a film, stupid things happen. God only knows what would happen if you tried to convert *this* unstoppable barf-fest into a film. The FBI would probably have to get involved. There's a chance you could consider it an act of terrorism.)

I'm briefly going to freak out here about Madison Hartner. It turns out she doesn't date any of the Pittsburgh Steelers, or even a college student. Two weeks before school ended, she started dating *Allan McCormick*. He's this gaunt little gothy dork with worse skin than mine and eerily short arms and legs and a big haggard face that doesn't match the rest of his body. Actually, I guess he's not a gothy dork anymore. In February, he stopped playing Magic cards in the morning with Scott Mayhew and transitioned into a straight-up smart kid. But still. It turns out Madison Hartner has no dating standards *at all*.

So I guess there's a chance I could have gotten with her that whole time, if I had spent more time working it in the cafeteria and less time in Mr. McCarthy's office.

Although on second thought there's no way that's true.

Speaking of Mr. McCarthy, it turns out he's not a stoner, and he doesn't put marijuana in his own soup. When we got high, it was actually from the cookies that Earl brought to school for lunch that day. Maxwell's then-girlfriend made them for him, and they contained an inordinate amount of pot. Earl found out about this months after the fact, when he and Maxwell were randomly beating the shit out of each other.

This was reassuring. Also, it fit what I know about the world of drugs. Because the truth is, a teacher who is high literally all the time would not be interesting and unpredictable and fact-oriented like Mr. McCarthy. Instead, that teacher would be eating things constantly and then failing to make intelligible sentences.

As for Earl, we've hung out a few times since Thuyen's Saigon Flavor. Now he works at a Wendy's. He's too short to work the register, so that fills him with rage. He's still living at home but he's saving up to get his own apartment.

It's weird, hanging out and not doing films. We sit around and talk about our lives instead. I've sort of gotten to know him better during the past few months than I did during the years that we were making Gaines/Jackson films, and let me tell you this: Earl is fucking insane.

Secretly I have this hope, which I know is stupid, that I'll get out of film school and make some big successful film right away and be able to start a production company and hire Earl as the co-president. But that's definitely not going to happen. In fact, if we ever work together again, it's more likely to be at a Wendy's. I can't believe I just typed that. That is the most depressing thing I have ever typed in my life. It's probably true, though.

I guess I want to write one more thing about Rachel. Rachel died about ten hours after Mom and I left the hospital. She had a weird Jewish funeral service at our synagogue and no one, thank God, asked me to say anything, and they didn't show the film that we made. Rachel was cremated, and her ashes were sprinkled in Frick Park, where apparently she loved to go as a kid. She ran away there once when she was seven—not because she was trying to get away from home, but apparently just because she wanted to live in the woods and be a squirrel.

It was weird to be learning something new about her even after she had died. Somehow it was also reassuring, though. I don't know why.

Maybe I should try to put her in my next film. I don't know. Honestly? I don't know what the hell I'm talking about.

FIN

Acknowledgments

This weird little book had many midwives, too many to be acknowledged here. But I will give explicit and impossible-to-overstate thanks to Maggie Lehrman, my editor and friend, who gave me superb and superbly modulated guidance from conception to completion, and without whom this book quite literally would not exist. I thank Matt Hudson, my erstwhile agent and also friend, who was somehow able to interest numerous important people in a very profane manuscript about boys who make homages to Werner Herzog and a girl who has cancer. I want to thank my parents, sisters, and grandma in advance for the times they will have to answer the question, "So, is that your family?" (No, it is not.) Finally, I am thankful for Tamara, who loves this book, and whom I love.

Jesse Andrews

is a novelist and musician. He has worked previously as a travel writer, tour guide, and receptionist at a German youth hostel. Jesse was born and raised in Pittsburgh, Pennsylvania, and is a graduate of Schenley High School and Harvard University. He has also lived in San Sebastián, Spain; Berlin, Germany; Boston, Massachusetts; and Brooklyn, New York, where he currently makes his home. It was not until college that he even made out with a girl for more than five minutes. *Me and Earl and the Dying Girl* is his first novel. You can visit him online at www.jesseandrews.com.

This book was art directed by Chad W. Beckerman. The chapter openers were designed by Meagan Bennett, and the character illustrations were illustrated by Brian Levy. The text is set in 10.75-point Adobe Garamond, a typeface based on those created in the sixteenth century by Claude Garamond. Garamond modeled his typefaces on ones created by Venetian printers at the end of the fifteenth century. The modern version used in this book was designed by Robert Slimbach, who studied Garamond's historic typefaces at the Plantin-Moretus Museum in Antwerp, Belgium.